LOYAL DISLOYALTY

Also by Jeffrey Ashford

LOYAL DISLOYALTY

Jeffrey Ashford

ST. MARTIN'S PRESS NEW YORK

Library of Congress Cataloging-in-Publication Data

Ashford, Jeffrey, 1926—
  Loyal disloyalty / Jeffrey Ashford.
    p.   cm.
  ISBN 0-312-19918-X
  I. Title
  PR6060.E43L64   1999
  823'914—dc21   98-47511
                                               CIP

First published in Great Britain by Collins Crime, an imprint of HarperCollins*Publishers*

First U.S. Edition: January 1999

10 9 8 7 6 5 4 3 2 1

LOYAL DISLOYALTY

CHAPTER 1

Serena lowered her voice as she leaned slightly forward. 'Why do men like tying women down to the bed before they . . . you know what?'

Diana's sharp surprise was caused not by the question, but by the fact that her sister should have asked it; normally, Serena found sex far too embarrassing to discuss even obliquely.

The waitress came up to their table. 'Would you like some more patisseries, madam? And perhaps some fresh coffee?'

Serena sat back and looked at Diana. 'How about another éclair?'

'Thanks, but I won't.'

'I thought you liked them?'

'I do.'

'One more can't possibly do any harm.'

'That's what you think.' She didn't think anything of the sort, of course, Diana decided, cheerfully aware of how uncharitable she was being; had they both had another, Serena's greed, especially for chocolate, would have been camouflaged.

'Well, I'm going to have another and then skip pud at lunch.' She turned to the waitress. 'One éclair and some more coffee.'

'Thank you, madam.' All the waitresses were middle aged and trained to offer the obsequious politeness to be expected in somewhere called – with that strange love of bogus antiquity – Ye Olde Tea Rooms.

As soon as the waitress was out of earshot, Diana said: 'Why your sudden interest in bondage?'

Serena answered irritably, obviously regretting having asked the question. 'Forget it.'

'Has Tom been tying you down before leaping aboard?'

'What a foul thing to say! Sometimes I don't begin to understand you.'

'Not very surprising. Mother once told me that we were so different that if she hadn't had the upset of bearing both of us, she'd never have believed we were sisters.'

'When did she say that?'

'Aeons ago; when we were kids. I think I'd just hit you and Mother was comparing my tomboy approach with your ladylike demeanour.' It hadn't been aeons ago, it had been when Serena had announced her engagement. 'You're not going to believe this,' their mother had said, 'because I don't. Nevertheless, your sister is going to marry that pompous little snob who's at least twice her age.'

The waitress returned, collected up the dirty plates and the empty coffee pot, put down on the table a filled coffee pot and an éclair on a scallop-shaped dish. Serena used tongs to put the éclair on her plate. She sliced off the end with her fork, ate with greedy pleasure.

Life really was bloody unfair, Diana thought. Serena not only had youth (she was ten years younger; her mother had considered christening her Surprise), looks, and wealth, she could eat as many chocolate éclairs as she wanted yet not put on an ounce of flab. Conscious that it was a sense of jealousy which prodded her to continue with a subject Serena clearly wished to forget, but unwilling to forgo the pleasure of returning to it, she said: 'So, now tell all. Why the curiosity?'

Serena wiped her mouth with a paper serviette, hesitated, then said: 'I was watching a film on the telly last night and the man tied down the woman to a bed before he . . .' She did not finish.

'Before he screwed her?' Diana was gratified to note Serena's increased unease at such direct speech. 'Dick used to say that variety was really the spice of sex, not life. But since his interests never led in that direction, like you I can't understand. After all, I've always understood that much of the pleasure is supposed to be supplied by a partner's imaginative moves, so why should he deprive himself? You'll have to ask Tom if he can explain.'

Serena abruptly changed the conversation. 'How is Richard?' She made a point of never using a diminutive.

'As far as I know, he's all right,' she answered, suddenly defensive.

Serena seized the chance to embarrass as much as she had been embarrassed. 'You haven't seen him recently?'

'Last weekend when he took Melly out for the day.'

'You let him do that?'

'What on earth do you expect? He is her father.'

'Does he ever take her back to his home?'

'Once or twice.'

'So Amelia's met the woman?'

'Yes.'

'What does she think of her?'

'I haven't been told.'

'You've not tried to find out?'

'Of course not.'

'It would be too awful if Amelia liked her, wouldn't it?'

'Why?'

'Well, I mean . . . I imagine you make very certain you don't meet the woman?'

'Why should I worry?'

'But surely it would be so humiliating to look at her and know . . .'

'The only person who'd be humiliated would be she, after I'd finished telling her just what I think of her for busting up our marriage and causing Melly so much distress. She used to be such an up-and-go child, now she spends much of her time just mooning around.'

'Men never think of that end of things.'

'When a young bimbo waves her goodies, men only have room for one thought.'

'That's why I'm so lucky with Thomas. He's not like that.'

The outrageous hypocrisy of that remark made Diana mentally blink; Serena had waved, Tom had thought.

7

'I know how to cheer Amelia up. She can come and spend a weekend with us.'

'That would be fun for her,' Diana said, trying to sound enthusiastic.

'I read recently that there's a new theme park which is wonderful for children. I'll take her there.'

'It's up in the Midlands, not far from Birmingham.'

'Really? That would be rather a long way to go, wouldn't it? Still, there's always plenty to do at Farthingstone. And Thomas is thinking of buying some horses; if he does, she can ride.'

'I rather doubt that any horse which will carry him will be of much use to Melly.'

'He's not fat.'

That depended on one's viewpoint. Seen sideways on . . . 'Melly's only six. The most she could cope with would be a very small pony.'

'I'll tell Thomas to buy one for her.'

This was Serena being the *grande dame*. Diana said sweetly: 'I'm surprised Tom's thinking of starting riding at his age – it can be very dangerous to old bones. Still, it is a useful way of getting to know the county crowd.'

'That's not the reason he's thinking of having horses.'

'Of course not. What makes you think I was suggesting anything of the sort? It was just a remark made en passant.'

'Then you ought to stop and think more before you speak.'

'Dick used to say that thinking was the death of good conversation.'

'That's the kind of thing he would say. Half the time I couldn't understand what he was getting at.'

'An advantage not to be lightly dismissed.'

Serena finished her éclair. She sniffed the coffee she had just poured, sipped it, added another spoonful of sugar. Her tone changed and became light, almost coy. 'Have you noticed anything new?'

The watch, Diana thought. So casually revealed when they'd first met. Serena had obviously lost patience at the lack of comment concerning it. 'I was taught at school that

I should notice something new every day, but so far I've drawn a blank.'

'Then here's your chance to do as you should.' Serena pulled back the left-hand sleeve of her lightweight coat and held her wrist so that the gold watch was clearly visible. 'Thomas gave it to me for our wedding anniversary.'

'What fun! Swatches are all the rage.' The moment she'd spoken, Diana accepted that she'd gone too far. She hastened to make amends. 'Just rank envy speaking! It really is very lovely. May I have a close look?'

Serena hesitated, as if wondering whether to forgive such *lèse-majesté*, then finally held her hand out across the table. 'It's a Boucheron.'

Diana humbly said all the right things.

Serena withdrew her hand. 'I mustn't be late because we're having lunch with the Brierleys. D'you know them?'

'Only by name.'

'He's asked Thomas to join the committee of the society he's just formed and of which he's chairman.'

'What's it in aid of?'

'Preserving traditional rural England in the face of modern farming.'

'Sounds like a lost cause.'

'Which is why the society's motto is: Tall oaks grow from tiny acorns.'

'Provided the squirrels don't get there first.'

'Why do you always have to sneer at everything?'

'Do I?'

'I suppose it's understandable, considering what's happened.' She beckoned the waitress across. 'The bill.'

The waitress made it out, folded it up, put it down on the table at Serena's side. 'Thank you for coming here today, madam.'

As the waitress left, Serena picked up the bill and unfolded it. 'This place is becoming impossibly expensive.'

'We'd better go halves, then.'

'Not when I invited you,' Serena snapped. 'All I was saying was, they seem to think we're made of money.' She opened her crocodile-skin handbag, brought out a purse. 'Tipping is so demeaning to everybody concerned,' she added, as she slid a ten-pence piece under her plate.

Her sister knew how to feel not too demeaned, Diana thought.

CHAPTER 2

Richard Adeane stretched across the desk to take the newly typed itinerary of the coming visit of three German journalists. 'Thanks a lot, Anne, for staying on to get this done.'

'For you, any time, any place, any how.' She grinned, left the room swinging her hips.

An offer that undoubtedly would be withdrawn the moment there was any suggestion of its being accepted. Through her young eyes, he must appear old enough to need a crutch. He swivelled the chair round until he could tap out instructions on the desktop computer's keyboard to call up the *aide-mémoire*. He checked. Air flights booked and tickets sent by recorded post; two cars detailed to be at the airport to meet the incoming flight; hotel bookings made and confirmed; welcome at the factory organized (Steve still had to be reminded that these were Germans so he must start his speech of welcome by saying Germany was his favourite foreign country, not France); four hours' free time for shopping, having received written notes on where to obtain the best buys (underwear in silk was very popular. It was just possible this was for wives); dinner at the Ostler's Arms, much more upmarket than the name suggested, hosted by the chairman (aka Pompous Prat); the following morning, two hours at Brand's Hatch, driving Lantairs as fast as they liked, provided they'd signed blood chits absolving the company from any and all liability (why were motoring correspondents some of the most incompetent drivers in the world?); cars to take them back to the airport . . .

He switched off the computer, swivelled his chair back, wrote a note to Anne that it was OK to distribute copies of the itinerary to all interested parties. This would be the first visit from Germany and he wondered how they'd react to a car which had been designed in 1951 and then carefully kept in that era? Italians loved Lantairs because they loved all cars which offered fun. The French treated them with patronizing condescension because it was treason to be seen to admire anything from across La Manche, nevertheless they bought them because women found them sexy. So the Germans . . . By reputation, they sought power and progress and saw little merit in nostalgia, but one never knew; until one found out.

He pushed his chair back and crossed to the window, looked out. Immediately opposite, on the other side of the road, was the garden of the vicarage; it was a mass of colour. The vicar clearly was a keen and successful gardener. He wasn't. He remembered the day when he'd dragged up a mesembryanthemum, misidentifying it as a weed. Diana had told him that he might well become blue from cold, red from anger, even yellow from fear, but he'd never have green fingers . . . He wondered why he so often recalled a moment of no consequence when he did his damndest to forget even those of great consequence? Presumably on the same basis that if one set out not to think of fish, one inevitably envis-aged shoal after shoal . . .

He retrieved his mackintosh from the old-fashioned coat stand and left the office. The lift was waiting, but he chose to go down the stairs. Exercise had become a key word. That morning, when in his pyjamas, Patricia had told him that he was developing a middle-aged tum. Very conscious of their difference in ages, he'd denied the charge as he'd sucked in his stomach, squared his shoulders, and tried to feel thirty. It was astonishing how ridiculous even an intelligent man could become in the face of a younger woman . . .

He left the building and crossed to the far end of the car park and his Peugeot 205. Senior staff were provided with Lantairs which they were expected to use at all times, junior staff had to provide their own transport. An arrangement that suited neither party.

He backed, turned, and drove up to the gates where the gateman motioned to him to wait. As the traffic rumbled past, his mind, fired by that memory of the mesembryanthemum, went walkabout. Was there any one set of circumstances which now could, with hindsight, be seen to mark the point at which the marriage had begun to founder?

They'd both had definite ideas on almost all subjects and so had often disagreed, but they had learned to live with this. Diana's pregnancy had been a time of physical unpleasantness for her and strain for him, since sex had come to a full stop, but they'd survived. Amelia had squealed and squalled and left Diana exhausted . . .

A shout brought him back to the present; the gateman was waving him out. He engaged first and drove forward, only to have to brake sharply because he'd left things too late. A sour comment on life. Missed opportunities only recognized as such after they had been missed . . . A stream of traffic passed, then there was another break, thanks to lights a quarter of a mile back. He drove out.

Amersford was a town which had once possessed character, but this had been lost to blind, greedy development. A shopping centre had replaced the cattle market, a block of offices, the corn market; supermarkets and chain stores had forced the family shops into liquidation and now there was not a single independent grocer, butcher, baker, wine merchant or hardware store to offer quality and interested service. Much of High Street had been pedestrianized, enforcing a one-way system on surrounding roads which so defied logic that at one point a motorist wishing to drive north found himself heading south.

Adeane turned into Rander's Road and slowed, searching for a parking space; luck provided one close to home. He climbed out, locked up, and walked on to No. 17, an architecturally neutered semi-detached, built between the wars. To look at it was to remember the mellow charm of Turnbull Farm; which was to dislike No. 17 a little more.

He unlocked the front door and stepped into the hall. There was no sound of television from the front room, so Patricia was not yet back from work. The emptiness depressed him and he went past the stairs and into the kitchen, where he poured himself a drink. He crossed to the refrigerator for ice and noticed how bare the shelves were. Supper was once again going to be out of the deep freeze. Patricia always claimed she didn't have the time to cook; the truth was, she simply couldn't be bothered to do so. Being a housewife was not where her abilities lay . . .

He had returned to the hall when he heard the click of the front-gate latch. He opened the door as Patricia held out the key to insert it in the lock. 'Snap!'

'What . . . ? You startled me!'

'Humble apologies.'

She replaced the key in her purse, purse in handbag; she stepped inside. He kissed her, to find her unresponsive. She was the first to agree that there were times when she was turned on and times when she wasn't.

'I've had a really lousy day,' she said fretfully.

He closed the front door. She could milk life dry of its pleasures, but found it very difficult to cope with even its minor stresses.

'That bitch chewed me up for something that wasn't my fault.'

'That bitch being Mary?'

'Who else?'

Mary, office manager, was middle aged, very earnestly married, and totally loyal to management; small wonder that she and Patricia had taken an instant dislike to each other. 'I've just poured myself a drink, so what can I get you to wash away the taste of work?'

'A whisky . . . Why doesn't the silly old cow get her facts right?'

Even if Mary did work for a newspaper, he thought that she was the kind of woman who always got her facts right. 'Go into the sitting-room and I'll bring you one very large whisky.'

'One day I'll tell her what I really think of her,' she said, as she turned away.

He was pouring out the whisky when the telephone in the hall rang. He put down the bottle and glass, hurried through the kitchen and into the hall to see Patricia lift the receiver. He waited, but when she said, 'I was thinking of ringing you,' he returned to the kitchen.

He carried the whisky to where she stood and pointed at the small table to ask whether she wanted the drink there; she nodded and he put the glass down. As he entered the sitting-room, he heard her say, 'Oh, no, Caroline!' and knew the call was going to be a long one.

When she entered the room, she said: 'That was Caroline.'

'So I gathered.'

'There's no need to be like that. She's charming.'

'If you say so.'

'What a mournful bastard you can be.'

'Mournful, certainly, illegitimate, never. I'm sufficiently old-fashioned to have been born in wedlock.'

'Now you're being all pompous.' She drank most of what remained in her glass. 'Caroline's had an idea.'

'In the face of so unusual an event, it's no wonder the call was a long one.'

'God, you're being even more of a bore than usual!' She drained her glass. 'I want another.'

He collected both their glasses and refilled them in the kitchen, returned. As he handed her a glass, she said: 'Caroline's suggesting we all go to France for the day through the tunnel.'

'I thought Fred disliked the French almost as much as the Welsh.'

'That's only because they made him try to learn Welsh at school. Carry's been told about a restaurant near Calais which is specially mentioned in the Michelin guide and the food's out of this world.'

'Ambrosia meunière.'

'You really are in one of your bloody moods.'

'Sorry.'

'Wouldn't it be great to go and find out if the food's as good as it's supposed to be?'

'If it's special, so will the prices be.'

'As Carry said, there's no point in going to France and having fish and chips.'

'Quite. But one can still find as good a meal at a small, family-run restaurant at a fraction of the cost.'

'You always reduce everything to money.'

'Only the rich or the poor don't have to.'

'We wouldn't have to scrimp and scrape if you didn't give her so much.'

He was surprised it had taken this long to raise the matter of the allowance he gave Diana.

'She's got a job.'

'Only part time. And Amelia has to be fed and clothed.'

'Always Amelia. If you're going to go on giving her so much, why don't you find a job that pays a decent wage?'

He wondered how large the wage had to be before she would accept it as decent?

As he lay in bed and listened to Patricia's slow, deep breathing deepen, he tried to remember Virgil's description of women which he'd carefully learned at school at a time when women were a subject for giggling uncertainties. *Varium et* . . . Irritatingly, the rest was lost to time. In Italian (a linguist, he!): *La donna è mobile*. In English: Never bet on what a woman's going to do next. For most of the evening, she'd been in a bad temper and he'd been certain that she'd make it plain – in one of the many ways women employed – that bed was going to be for sleeping. Instead of which, she'd initiated the lovemaking . . .

He gently rested his right hand on her naked body. Would science, philosophy, or thaumatology, ever be able to explain why one woman filled a man's mind with lusty thoughts and another, perhaps objectively more attractive, did not? His first sight of Patricia in the offices of the *Amersford Gazette* had had him thinking, even before she'd looked in his direction, that she could count up to sixty-nine very quickly . . .

Life, as one would-be sage had written, was such a chaos of ifs that one's path through it could only be marked out with hindsight. If he'd not been so psychologically shattered by redundancy, if Diana had been able to understand that even the strong could become weak . . . He'd married her, knowing that her warmth, friendliness, and reluctance to criticize, did not betoken a softness of character – there were certain standards which, however unusual this had become, she honoured with steely certainty, and loyalty was one such; loyalty to one's family, friends, responsibilities.

He'd always believed himself strong, but when he'd been made redundant, he'd suffered feelings of inadequacy, guilt, and as the redundancy money trickled away, panic. From the beginning, Diana had been briskly confident that he'd find another job and refused to accept the possibility he might not; because of this, because she'd considered he was not fighting as he should, she'd been unable to understand the despair that had gripped him. He'd needed sympathy, she'd offered criticism. If his mind had been clear, he'd have realized that whilst a little sympathy would have helped, too much would have fuelled his sense of hopelessness; that it was her love and loyalty speaking, not her growing contempt for him. But his mind had been fogged and there had been rows which had become bitter; he had said things which had been designed to hurt and she had been hurt . . .

He'd left home on foot to save the cost of petrol (ironic, this, since within days he'd recklessly spent money on Patricia) to go to the library to check the day's papers for possible jobs. The route he'd chosen had taken him past the *Gazette*'s offices and an impulse – which at the time had seemed unaccountable; later, could not have been more easily explained – had taken him inside. If Patricia had not been working at the information desk that morning . . .

He'd not tried to hide the fact he was married, but had explained that Diana couldn't understand how he felt. (Since Patricia hadn't laughed at that cliché, he should have recognized that she lacked a developed sense of humour.) Patricia had been careless about reasons; her sole concern was to enjoy life . . .

Women possessed a sixth sense that was always in 'Go' mode. Only days after there had been cause for the question, Diana had asked him if he were having an affair with another woman. He'd never been a good liar when his conscience was involved and she had contemptuously disbelieved his denial; in the end, he'd finally admitted the truth. Her sense of loyalty owed and due was such that she hadn't even tried to understand and through understanding forgive . . . If only she'd learned that strength could be as flawed as weakness.

He moved his hand until it brushed Patricia's pert left breast. She might lack Diana's strengths, but that could be an advantage.

CHAPTER 3

Turnbull Farm had been a working home until, as Amersford expanded, all the land had been sold for development. Now, with a garden of just under three-quarters of an acre, it presented a visual anomaly – a seventeenth-century farmhouse, so matured by time that it seemed to belong to the land, surrounded by twentieth-century urban homes which would never be anything but eyesores.

Adeane drove off the road and parked in front of the garage, an ancient wooden shed with a list. He walked slowly along the gravel path, remembering the day they'd come to view the house. They'd found all the features they'd ever wanted – beams galore, inglenook fireplace, some original floorboards over a foot wide, a door with a lock made from wood, a shoe that, probably in the eighteenth century, had been bricked up in the wall for good luck and discovered only a few years before, the typical long, sharply sloping peg-tile roof . . . The asking price had been above their agreed maximum. Agreements were made to be broken. When they'd moved in, they'd both felt the house was welcoming them. On the day he'd moved out . . . That was something he tried to forget.

The brick path took him round the corner of the house to the front door, solid wood, grey and lightly striated by the centuries.

Diana opened the door and he kissed her on one cheek. Most, but not all, of the time their relationship had become that of two people who never sought out the other's company, but accepted it when there was cause to do so with pleasant neutrality.

She was looking tired, he thought; there seemed to be

extra lines about the eyes, adding a year, or two. Even when younger and her face unlined, she'd not been beautiful in the conventional sense, as was Serena. Her features were too strong and her chin too square; her black hair lacked any hint of a wave and she favoured no particular style; plumpness was always just around the corner; even her lustrous, dark-brown eyes were a shade too large . . . Yet when he'd met the two sisters for the first time, it had been she who had claimed his immediate attention.

'Do I look an absolute fright? I'm wearing this because I was cleaning the stove.' She undid the knot behind her back and slipped the apron over her head.

'I wasn't staring. My mind was walking back in time.'

'I thought you've always said that that's more dangerous than skating on no ice?'

'I'm full of wisdom to which I never listen . . . Is Melly ready?'

'She's not back yet. You'd better come in and wait.'

He stepped into the hall which, because of the steep pitch of the long roof, was triangular shaped. 'Back from where?'

'Amy. It's her birthday and Melly wanted to take the present this morning. Which reminds me, if you would see that Melly's back by four, which is when the party starts?'

'I'll do that.'

There was a pause which she broke. 'Would you like a coffee?'

'If it's not too much trouble when you're cleaning the stove.'

'I've just about finished.'

It was strange to be a guest in what had been his own home, his wife the hostess. He followed her into the small kitchen at the far end of the hall, automatically ducking under the low lintel. 'I see you've redecorated.'

'I needed something to do.'

He wondered why, when she had the part-time job and Melly to look after, but received the unspoken command not to ask. They had always been receptive to each other's thoughts, never certain whether this was due to ESP or emotional insight. 'And the fridge is new.'

'The old one packed up and the engineer told me it just wasn't worth repairing.'

He stared through the nearer window, to the left of the refrigerator. 'The garden's a picture.'

'Thanks to the weather, I've been able to do a lot. What's more, I've managed to persuade Melly to give me a hand from time to time.' She measured ground coffee with a spoon, screwed the two parts of the coffee maker together, set them on the cooker and lit the gas. 'I've no chocolate biscuits to offer you. If they're in the house, I eat them. And even without that temptation, I've put on four pounds in the last week. Maybe even a little more,' she added unwillingly.

'Console yourself with the thought that it doesn't show.'

'I always find it difficult to believe my own lies.'

'Why the panic? Are doctors still trying to get everyone on to a starvation diet?'

'I had coffee with Serena yesterday and after seeing her, I always become very conscious of my bulges ... Since I can't offer you a biscuit, how about a sandwich with a home-grown tomato?'

'Thanks, but I cooked myself a full breakfast and it's still there.'

'*You* cooked it?' She immediately regretted having asked the question and turned away, vexed, to reach for the sugar.

He wondered what she'd think if he told her how seldom Patricia cooked any meal? Before they'd married, she'd made it clear that it was going to be a partnership, not a takeover on his part, but unless ill, she'd never expect him to have any part in the cooking.

The coffee machine hissed and she turned off the gas, poured coffee into two mugs, added sugar in one and milk. As she passed him a mug, she said: 'Let's go and sit.'

He followed her through the hall to the sitting-room; despite the fact that the floor had been lowered by several inches, he had to duck to pass under the central beam. As he sat, he said: 'The loose covers are wearing well.'

'So they should, considering what they cost! Do you remember ... ?' She came to an abrupt halt. Memories needed to be sanitized before being spoken. 'How's work going?'

'Same as ever.'

'What does that mean?'

'The actual work is fine, the office politics remain juvenile, irrational, and counterproductive.'

'How long did it take you to think that up?'

'Not nearly as long as I've had to wait for the chance to use it.'

She smiled.

'If the rest of industry were run with the same degree of intelligence, we'd still be wondering if a wheel could ever be of any practical use.'

'I thought you've always said that Lantair's success depends on producing a car that's so out of date it taps the wells of nostalgia? Or is that just another laboured apophthegm?'

'Has anyone ever told you that sometimes you're bad for the ego? Lantair's success rests entirely on a car that's fifties outside, even if parts of the inside are state of the art. But however much nostalgia appeals to a select few, it's got to find a wider market if the company's to stay viable. That calls for publicity, especially in overseas markets.'

'Which is where you come in?'

'Which is where I come in, but keep finding the going sticky because of Emms.'

'Emms being your boss?'

'My consultant. He retired a couple of years ago when I took over from him.'

'If he's only a consultant, how can he be that much of a cross?'

'Because he has the chairman's ear and spends his life shouting down it. He was one of the five original employees when Sir Edward started the company and has grown equally old and cantankerous. When he became too gaga for an active position, he was made PRO by the chairman who thinks publicity is rather infra dig. When I joined the department it was virtually moribund, but every suggestion I made to bring it back to life was squashed flat by him on the grounds that if it hadn't been done before, there was no need to do it now. When he retired, I reckoned I'd the go light to get things changed, but it turned out he'd only half retired because he stayed on the books as a consultant.'

'And sticks his oar in?'

'A double bank of oars. Virtually every alteration I've made has been damned by him.'

'Has he managed to thwart you very often?'

'Only occasionally and only over matters that weren't important enough for me to do full battle. The board has some old fogies on it who blindly do as Sir Edward says, but there are just enough younger members who understand that you don't sell anything just because it's good, you sell it because you persuade people to believe it's good. They support what I do because since I've been PRO, sales have gone up, especially in Europe, and profits have increased, but it gets so bloody wearing, having to fight through cobwebs to change anything.'

'Surely you secretly enjoy the need to overcome resistance?'

'Unfair! . . . Enough of the drama, let's move on to farce. You said you saw Serena yesterday?'

'We had coffee at the tea rooms.'

'Coffee only or coffee with?'

'With a chocolate éclair.'

'Hence the needless worry about your weight! How was your narcissistic sister?'

'Dressed as if she'd just come off a catwalk.'

'Where more appropriate for her to strut?'

'Your sense of humour doesn't improve.'

'Just so long as it doesn't become any worse . . . Was she good company?'

'Expectant company. She worked very hard to show me the watch Tom's given her for their wedding anniversary. It's a rather lovely gold Boucheron. I told her I'd thought it was a Swatch.'

He laughed. 'I guess she didn't think much of your sense of humour!'

'She ought to know better than to expect me to exclaim

23

in wonder . . . Look, there's something concerning her over which you can help. She's going to ask Melly for a weekend and I can't think how to get Melly out of it.'

'Is there any particular reason why you want to?'

'She can't stand Tom.'

'That shows my daughter has inherited my good taste. Why doesn't she like him?'

'I've tried more than once to get her to explain, but all she'd say is, he makes her kind of shiver inside.'

'D'you think he's tried something with her?'

'Good God, no! If he had, she'd have told me at once.'

'I don't know that that's quite so sure. Children can feel the incident's partially their own fault and that makes them secretive and frightened.'

'I'm certain there's been nothing like that.'

'Then it's just an instinctive dislike. Children can be very sharp judges of character.'

'Have you any idea how I can get her out of staying there?'

'Try suspected mumps. That'll turn Tom into a quaking jelly, since he views even colds with horror, and he'll cancel the invitation.'

'That's quite a good idea.'

'I'm full of them. It's execution that's always my problem.'

She drained her mug. 'Serena said something over coffee that astonished me.'

'Because it was intelligent?'

'She wanted to know why men sometimes tie women down to the bed before screwing them.'

'She did what? Amazement is far too weak an emotion.'

'I know. Normally she's so twee she becomes all coyly embarrassed if birds and bees are mentioned in the same sentence.'

'So what on earth provoked the question?'

'She'd been watching a film on telly and the hero – or the villain – tied the woman down to the bed before jumping her. Serena was certain I'd know what made a man want to do that, but when I thought about it, I discovered I'd no idea. So you tell me why a man likes to immobilize a woman?'

'To prevent her reading a book while he's panting away.'

'It's a serious question.'

'Then a serious answer is, that's not my scene and I don't know.'

'You disappoint me.'

'If you were tied down, you'd disappoint me.'

It was an unfortunate remark. It left them in silence, each deep in thought.

The carriage clock on the top shelf of the small bookcase to the right of the fireplace struck eleven. Diana looked towards the door. 'I told Melly to be back by half past ten and she promised faithfully she would be.'

'It may not be her fault. Amy's mother probably couldn't drive her back dead on time.'

'She's on her bike.'

'Is that wise?'

'It's only just down the road. And she did so want to go under her own steam.'

'Maybe, but . . .'

'One can't keep them in cotton wool.'

'I accept that, but surely there are some risks she's got to be shielded from until she's older and can appreciate them for what they are. There have been some pretty horrible rapes recently.'

'But not in places like this . . . That's being stupid! There's no such thing as a safe area any longer because no one has the courage to bring back law and order.' She stood. 'I'll ring.' She left, to go into the hall.

He listened, suffering a growing sense of tension. The modern world set parents an impossible question to answer – how slack to hold the reins? He heard Diana say hullo. If Amelia had left in time to arrive home at ten-thirty . . . Then Diana said: 'No, of course it's not your fault if she never told you. I'll have words when she gets back! But if you will send her packing right away . . .'

He relaxed.

CHAPTER 4

As did anyone who had to deal continuously with human tragedy, WPC Holman normally managed to disassociate herself from the victim's suffering; but as she parked in front of the semi-detached in the middle of the housing estate in north Bledstone, she vainly wished herself anywhere but where she was. Rape had become a distressingly familiar crime, but rape a week before a marriage, which had caused the wedding to be postponed (for which read cancelled, because the prospective bridegroom was a selfish, weak bastard) and left the bride-to-be with severe internal injuries that might mean she could never have children, possessed an added and extra horror which pierced Holman's defence and left her associating with the victim's physical and mental suffering.

She locked the car, crossed the pavement, opened the wrought-iron gate. The short path, made from imitation York stone, passed through the left-hand side of a typical suburban garden – clipped box hedge, pocket-handkerchief lawn, oblong flowerbed carefully weeded. The front door under the small porch had been recently varnished and the bell sounded chimes. Yet when Mrs Ritchie opened the door, her strained expression bore witness to the fact that a quiet, conscientious life lived honestly was no defence against evil.

''Morning, Mrs Ritchie,' Holman said, her briskness revealing her emotional strain. 'How's Eve?'

'Much the same.'

'Would it be all right to have another chat?'

'I suppose.'

Holman entered the tiny hall that smelled of furniture polish.

'You'd best go in there. I'll tell Eve.'

She went into the front room, immaculately tidy. It was not the first time she had known grief to provoke excessive cleaning and polishing; she presumed it was an attempt – even if not recognized as such – to 'clean away' what had happened.

A few minutes later, Eve entered. A natural blonde with a well-featured oval face, slender and shapely, she would have made a beautiful bride.

'Hullo, Eve. How are things?'

'All right.'

'Come and sit down and tell me what the specialist had to say.'

Eve sat, did not speak. Her eyes were focused inwards; she fidgeted her fingers together as she rested her hands in her lap.

'Are you beginning to heal?'

'It's not so painful. Only . . . only the specialist still can't say how things are going to be.'

Holman, who had two children, could not prevent herself wondering how she would have reacted had she had to face the possibility of childlessness. 'Medical people always tend to be very pessimistic; makes them seem so much cleverer when their patients recover completely,' she said, suffering a sudden, overwhelming, and totally unprofessional need to help morale, even if this meant giving false hope.

If Eve gained even the slightest help, she gave no indication of that fact.

'I'd like another chat if you're up to it. How d'you feel about it?'

She remained silent.

'I want you to tell me exactly what happened, from the moment you left your friend's house to catch the bus.'

'I told you.'

'That's right, more than once. But people don't always remember everything the first or even the second time. So maybe you'll recall something that until now you've completely forgotten and although it may seem very unimportant to you, it could help us a lot.'

'It was the dog. If there hadn't been the dog, I'd never have got into the car. It was like Annie's.'

Holman noted the fact that here possibly was fresh evidence, but did not interrupt to ask the breed of Annie's dog. The technique of interrogating someone who was emotionally disturbed had been altered and now the witness was often left to ramble on, no matter how confusedly, and only when the evidence was completed did the interrogator begin to put questions to illuminate, or determine the value of, what had been said.

Eve continued to speak with a growing fluency. Holman listened, sadly aware that despite what had happened, Eve did not appreciate that she'd shown a lack of common sense and foresight. But then who really did understand that the seemingly unimportant decision was often the most important the person would make in the whole of his or her life?

The hen party had not been the cheerful event to celebrate Eve's forthcoming marriage to Ron that had been intended. Jane had not come on her own, as planned, but with Yvette who, after drinking too much, told the company that she'd known Ron a couple of years before; known him very well indeed. Jane had tried to patch things up, but Eve, emotionally strung out, had called Yvette a lying bitch and said she wasn't going to stay another second. They'd tried to make her change her mind, but she wouldn't – she'd had more than one drink. Jane had offered to run her home by car. She'd refused, bracketing Jane with Yvette. She'd left the house to catch the last bus to east Bledstone, only to discover that she'd forgotten that on a Sunday the last one left at ten. As she'd stood at the bus stop, the rain had begun. Obviously, the sensible thing to do was return and accept the lift, but she'd told herself that she'd be damned if she'd afford Yvette the chance to sneer; she'd walk. The rain had increased and begun to soak through her coat. Miserably, she'd plodded on ... A passing car had stopped. The driver had leaned across to open the nearside window and as he'd done so, the dog had appeared, scrabbling at the glass, yapping as it did so. The man, having to shout to overcome the noise when the window was partially down, had offered her a lift. She knew the perils of accepting a lift from a stranger, but the rain showed no signs of abating, her coat would soon be sodden, her ankles were beginning to ache, terrible things happened to others, and dogs were owned by nice, kindly people . . .

They'd just passed the Marsham crossroads when he'd said his right foot was catching on something and he'd have to check what that was in case he had to brake suddenly. She'd taken small notice because she'd had the dog on her lap and was stroking it. He'd stopped and she'd been about to ask him why he'd called a bitch Rex when he'd reached out and pulled her sideways and clapped a cloth over her face that was soaked in something with a penetrating, acrid smell and which had begun to burn. She'd tried to fight, but the fumes had quickly caused her to lose consciousness.

When she'd come to, she'd been stripped naked, blind-folded and gagged with masking tape, her hands tied behind her back. He had subjected her to a prolonged and horrifying sexual ordeal, then pulled the rug from under her and left.

She'd staggered out of the small copse and on to the road. A car had come along in which had been a kind, practical couple. The wife had wrapped a coat around her and cradled her in her arms on the back seat as they'd driven home, where the husband had phoned for an ambulance and the police . . .

'You said the dog was like Annie's. What kind of dog does she own?'

'A West Highland White.'

'Well?' demanded the detective inspector, a thin, astringent man respected for his ability, but disliked for his character.

'I've learned one new thing, sir,' Holman replied. 'The dog was probably a West Highland White.'

'Not exactly a case-cracking piece of information.'

'It could be more important than it seems.'

'How so?'

'She said again that the dog was yapping and scrabbling at the car window. Initially she thought it probably wanted to spend a penny, but as soon as she was seated it settled on her lap. The man told her the dog's name was Rex, but she noticed that it was a bitch.'

'So what's the significance?'

'Unless he deliberately gave a bitch a male name, he didn't know its sex, in which case he could only have had it for a very short time. That suggests he stole it in order to provide the cover of normalcy that dogs give. It could well be worth finding out how many dogs went missing that day.'

'Have you any idea how many go missing every day?'

'Only one or two will have been West Highland Whites ... Find out where it's from and we could have a lead, provided he stole it from near his home. I know it's a bit of a long shot, sir, but surely it's worth following up? After all, this is the third known rape.'

'Pure assumption at this stage.'

Which didn't call for much intelligence to make, Holman thought.

'Make out a report. And check the spelling; I'm getting far too many that read as if written by illiterates.'

And that was as Irish as you could get! she thought, as she turned and left.

The DI carefully packed the bowl of his pipe with tobacco. Several folders were on his desk, but the only one he'd read so far that day concerned the rape. Mentally, he reviewed the known facts, searching yet again for something he had missed, even though convinced he had missed nothing. He lit the pipe, needing two matches to do so. Because of the many similarities with two other rapes which had occurred over the past months, in different parts of the country, it was presumed – whatever he'd said to the WPC – that the same man was the rapist. But putting together the known facts from all three cases failed to produce much of a picture. The first victim said the car had been red, the second blue or black, the third had no idea; none of them could identify make of car or any letter or number of the registration (a witness who might have seen one victim get into a car said the date letter put the car as twelve years old); each victim reported a small dog in the car. The man had worn a wide-brim hat which obscured part of the upper section of his head and he was variously described, the only consistent feature being a moustache (one of the easiest of disguises, yet remarkably efficient, except to a trained observer); speech was reported as smart, old-fashioned, perhaps a little false in accent, and there was a slight speech defect, but this was very difficult to describe. Each victim had been rendered unconscious with a chloroform pad, had regained consciousness to find herself stripped naked, blindfolded, gagged, and her hands tied behind her back; she had been subjected to rape and other sexual assaults. Forensic evidence was virtually nil; no semen, no traces on the victims' bodies, no traces in the immediate vicinities of the assaults. Obviously, the rapist had stripped, worn a condom, and afterwards carefully searched his victim's body to see he left behind none of his hairs. Driven by an appallingly perverted urge, yet he could foresee the dangers of succumbing to this without planning to make certain he left behind nothing that might identify him. This combination of lack of control and control was, according to a psychiatrist with considerable experience in sexual crimes, unusual; it suggested the rapist possessed considerable intelligence.

The DI's pipe had gone out and he relit it. WPC Holman was – for a woman – a fairly smart thinker. The dog might well have been stolen so that it could be used as a decoy. Which meant that, no matter how long a longshot, the attempt must be made to trace it by consulting police logs, questioning vets, reading through the small adverts in local newspapers and dog magazines . . .

The PC, temporarily seconded to CID, walked back from his car along the pavement to the elaborate wrought-iron gates. He opened these and continued up the twenty-foot gravel path to the front door of the large house. This was the smart part of Kington. He rang the bell. This was the part of Kington in which he'd live after he'd won the lottery.

The door was opened by a woman who, to judge from the style of her dress and make-up, was not as young as she hoped. She regarded his uniform without any of the wariness that it would have met in some of the other parts of town.

31

'Can I help you?' Her voice was tinged with condescension.

'Mrs Harvey?'

'Well?'

'Have you been running an advert in the local free press concerning a lost dog – a West Highland White?'

'You've found Mitzy?' she said, suddenly breathless.

'No, I'm afraid we haven't.'

Her disappointment was bitter. 'Then why are you asking?'

'Because you may be able to help us in a very important case . . . If I could ask you a few questions?'

She hesitated, then opened the door more fully. 'You'd better come in. And you can tell me why you're asking about Mitzy if you haven't found her.'

He stepped into a large hall. 'When did you lose your dog, Mrs Harvey?'

'Tuesday evening. I let her into the garden for a run, not knowing that the front gate had been left open by some stupid person who hadn't noticed a stone would stop it springing back.'

'What time was this?'

'It was getting dark. When I called and she didn't come in, I searched and found the open gate. I went out in my car and looked everywhere until after four o'clock . . . You'll know Mitzy when she's found because I had an identity tag implanted, even though it hurt her more than they promised it would . . .' She came to a stumbling halt, turned her head away.

He felt sorry for her. In the context of a series of appalling rapes, objectively a lost dog was nothing. Yet subjectively, she was suffering a very great loss.

CHAPTER 5

Every man was two men, the one he was and the one he wanted – and thought – himself to be; a very few were three men. For the very few, this third identity was hidden even from themselves for as long as that was possible, being a nightmare, too obscenely unspeakable even to recall with total disbelief. But sooner or later, perhaps for so slight a reason as a woman's wincing from brief pain, phoenix-like, reborn out of past fire, it reappeared. Then memory, anticipation, and imagination, became goads and changed the nightmare into a daydream, the obscenely unspeakable into the overwhelmingly desirable.

He had been christened Thomas Steven Jones. He'd only added Walker – his mother's maiden name – when he had attained success. For him, a double-barrelled surname denoted class.

After he'd first fought his way out of the world that had been his inheritance, he had deliberately blanked from his mind the memories of the indignities he had suffered. Then, as success had come his way, ironically he found himself retrieving those memories because now they offered pleasure, not pain. Those people whom he had especial cause to remember provided the greatest pleasure. Amos, the form bully, had beaten him up and left him a quivering, weeping wreck. Amos was in prison, on a life sentence. Molly had egged him on until he'd tried to run his hand up her legs and then she'd laughed and told him she'd only gone out with him for a joke and if he thought he was going to warm his fingers, he was suffering from woodworm in the brain. She had married a drunkard. Vera had looked down at him with contempt and said he'd better take up knitting, if he could ever find needles that didn't bend. She'd died young. Cecily, Elsa, Hester, Nancy, Tracy, all of whom had scorned him, all of whom, once he became wealthy, would have rushed had he but beckoned . . .

He stared through the large window as a Volvo brake came up the drive to stop by the raised, circular flowerbed. Serena climbed out, opened the front passenger door, brought out two parcels that clearly were light. More clothes. She had cupboards filled with clothes, yet still bought. It was an extravagance that recently had begun to irritate.

She walked towards the house. When her mother had heard about the engagement, she'd first been disbelieving, then contemptuously disapproving. Mrs Randall had the sense of God-given social superiority that had been so much more common in times of Empire. Yet what had she to be superior about when her husband had left her so hard up that she spent her widowhood in the company of church mice?

'I met Monica in town,' Serena said.

He looked along the fourteen feet length of the three-pedestal mahogany dining table. The thought had never occurred to him that, sitting at each end of the long table with three silver candelabra lined up along the centre and a cruet-stand in front of each of them, they were living a pretentious cliché. 'How is she?' He occasionally had difficulty with his sibilants.

'Very friendly.'

As well she should be, considering what he'd given to party funds in the past. As he'd said to the estate agent through whom he'd bought Farthingstone House (he'd thought of changing the name until assured it didn't refer to the smallest coin once in circulation), money might not buy friendship, but it certainly ensured people were friendly.

'She said we must have a meal with them and she'll check on her engagement diary and then ring to suggest a day.'

'It's about time they invited us back.'

'They're very busy socially and he is so often in London.' She finished the food on her plate. Immediately, Pablo, the

Filipino butler, wearing white coat, black trousers, and white gloves, picked up a silver dish from the sideboard and held it for her to help herself to some more devilled kidneys. When she'd taken what she wanted, she said to her husband: 'Have you any conferences coming up? I don't want to accept her invitation and then find you'll be away.'

'There will be one.'

'When?'

'Soon.'

'Then the organizers must know the date.'

'It's very much an ad hoc arrangement and dependent on the latest currency markets, which means it'll be fixed only at the very last moment.'

Pablo began to walk the length of the table, the dish in his right hand. Walker-Jones waved him away.

'If Monica suggests towards the end of next week, will that be all right?'

'As far as I can tell at the moment.'

'She says George is thinking of buying a new Bentley.'

'Thinking is as far as he'll ever get.'

'Why so?'

'Because I happen to know that right now he'd be hard pressed to afford the wheels and tyres, let alone the rest of the car.'

'How can you know that?'

'I keep my ears open.'

'Sometimes I think they're like those sound detectors in the last war . . .' She came to a stop as she remembered that he had noticeably large ears. Hastily, she added: 'Because they hear the slightest whisper.'

'Information is profit.'

Pablo refilled their glasses from the bottle of '78 Chambolle-Musigny. Walker-Jones drank, savouring the wine because he knew how much it had cost. 'I'm not going out after dinner, so we can have an early night.'

She mentally flinched. When he talked about 'an early night', she knew what to expect. Even a woman far less of a prude would have been dismayed by the prospect.

*   *   *

35

Men fantasized – women became the hunters, broke barriers rather than retreating from them – but most accepted that their fantasies could exist only in their minds or in pornography. He did not because he was too removed from the masses to be restrained by their inhibitions.

Of the three goads – memory, anticipation, imagination – he found memory usually the most potent. To recall the past was to paint the future in ever brighter colours . . .

He crossed to the drawers in the central built-in cupboard and from the bottom one brought out four lengths of silken cord, coloured red, bought in Istanbul. As he fondled these, he pictured her, waiting, apprehensive, frightened. She would have given much to escape his demands, but not the price he would have levied. She knew all too well that if she refused him, he would make certain she suffered by whatever means lay to hand.

He walked towards the bedroom door. Because she would not resist physically, his pleasure must be muted; but until he could once again find someone who would be desperate to resist him, he had to look to her for relief.

CHAPTER 6

Pamela Turner swore. She should have heeded the warnings of the garage. But their estimate for the proposed engine overhaul had promised to make mincemeat of the month's finances and several sizeable bills were due, so she'd decided to trust to luck. From the knocking, thumping sounds, she was going to need all the luck she could find.

The headlights picked out the next turning. Only two miles to go. 'Georgie Porgie,' she said aloud (the main registration letters were PIE), 'keep going until we reach home and I promise you an oil change.'

The engine died and the car rolled to a halt. With the baseless hope of a mechanical illiterate, she worked the starter several times, with total lack of success. She finally accepted that she was going to have to walk home in the rain and suffer her husband's juvenile humour – had she remembered to switch on? – before being towed in.

She picked up mackintosh, torch, and handbag from the front passenger seat, stepped out on to the road and slammed the door shut to express her feelings. She hurriedly put on her mackintosh and, not bothering to lock, began to walk. In was a dark night and she was grateful that Henry had suggested she should keep the torch in the car for emergencies; if, however, on her arrival home, he complimented himself at too great a length on his foresight, she'd crown him with a saucepan.

Headlights from behind lit up the road and elongated her shadow so that she seemed to have ten-league legs. She wondered how quickly she'd reach home if her legs were that long? They quickly foreshortened and the car went past, sending them racing into obscurity.

Should she stop at the pub in the village, phone home, and ask Henry to pick her up there? The trouble with that idea was that he found it so much easier to enter a pub than to leave it . . .

Another car approached from behind and as it drew near, the engine note dropped. Was the driver slowing down to offer help? Sir Galahad or one of her friends who'd recognized her from behind? Henry said that when she was annoyed, she walked like an ostrich in a bad temper.

The car drew alongside and stopped. She turned, raised the torch. The driver, leaning across the front passenger seat and winding down the window, was most definitely a stranger. None of their friends sported hats and moustaches that made them look like refugees from the thirties.

'Can I give you a lift?' he asked.

A small dog wriggled its way from under him to put its front paws on the top of the glass. It began to pant.

'It wants to get out,' he said, 'but if I let it, it'll make such a terrible muddy mess in the car.'

She strongly objected to a dog being referred to as an 'it'. Only a fool would ever consider letting a dog loose on a strange road on a night like this. And what sort of owner was he to worry about a bit of dirt? Her car sometimes resembled a ploughed field . . .

The dog began to climb out of the car. The driver grabbed it and jerked it back so forcefully it yelped.

'There's no need to hurt him,' she said indignantly.

'I just didn't want it leaping out of the car. Look, hop in and I'll drive you to wherever you want to go.'

It would have been a tempting offer had he not upset her by his manner. 'Thank you, but there's no need.'

'It'll be no bother.'

'My place is just down the road.'

'Even so, you'll get soaked.'

'I'm quite dry,' she said shortly, as several drops of water slid down her back. It annoyed her when people would not take no for an answer.

'You've nothing to fear from me and Toby.'

Ironically, the words which had been intended to allay

concern had the opposite effect. They reminded her that a man who was brutal to a dog was not to be trusted. 'I'm walking home.' She had kept the torch directed at him and saw his change of expression. She was not a woman who scared easily, but knew sudden alarm. She stepped back on to the grass verge, felt her shoes sink into the soft earth. If she had to run, she decided, conscious she was breathing more quickly than usual, she'd leave the shoes behind. At school, she'd been a noted runner and from the little she could see of him, he'd have trouble making the hundred yards in thirty seconds . . .

Distant lights appeared as a car rounded the right-hand corner half a mile ahead. The man abruptly straightened up, engaged first gear, and drove off.

Frightened off by the oncoming car? God Almighty, he really had been on the prowl! Grab the number . . . Because the conclusion shocked her, her reactions were delayed; the car was already quite a way away, the rain was blurring everything, and she could make out neither letters nor numbers.

She walked quickly past the pub to their cottage and as she opened the wooden gate and heard the dogs begin to bark, she knew a tremendous sense of relief. The two dogs and Henry met her in the hall. He did not increase his popularity when, as she fondled the dogs, he said: 'You look as if you've been swimming.'

'Georgie Porgie broke down and I've had to walk back.'

'Then it's lucky I – '

'Do you want me to hit you with something?'

'Not if it hurts too much.'

'Praise your marvellous forethought and you'll think I'm the Inquisition.'

'You're in a bit of a bate, aren't you?'

'If you can't judge I'm in one hell of a bate, you're very, very dense. What do we do about Georgie?'

'The garage shut hours ago so we'll have to tow it in with my car.'

'Only after I've had a shower, put on dry clothes, and had a really stiff whisky.'

He said uncertainly: 'I'm sorry, darling, but I had the last of the whisky whilst I was waiting for you to return . . .'

'My God, when I married you I didn't know what I was letting myself in for!'

'A real bargain.'

'Which, like all bargains, has a bloody big catch to it.'

'I'm really sorry about the whisky. Will a G and T do?'

'It'll have to, won't it?'

She went upstairs, followed by the dogs who were, for once, allowed into the bathroom. She stripped off and turned on the shower, juggled the controls until her patience gave out and she stepped into water which alternated between too hot and tepid.

He brought the drinks up while she was still in the shower. She reached out for a glass, drank, handed it back. 'I needed that!'

'Do you want your back soaped?'

'No.'

'Why not?'

'Because I know where that leads and we have to rescue Georgie Porgie as soon as possible in case the gypsies come along and pinch him.'

'They wouldn't be bothered.'

'You're being a real male bastard!' She turned off the shower. 'Pass me a towel, will you?'

He picked up a towel from the heated rail. 'I'll dry you.'

She stepped out of the shower, grabbed the towel from him, used her knee to fend off the Airedale which wanted to lick her dry.

'You're being a real spoilsport.'

'I'm being practical. Where's my glass?'

He handed it to her. 'Has something happened? I mean, apart from the car?'

'Why d'you ask?'

'When you got back, you seemed in a state. And it's not like you to drink so enthusiastically. I just wondered . . . Not had a row with Cindy, have you?'

She drained the glass, put it down by the side of the bath. 'After Georgie broke down, I began to walk back.' She dried

40

herself vigorously, then wrapped the towel around herself.

'And?'

She left the bathroom and walked across the landing into their bedroom, accompanied by the dogs who jumped up on to the bed. She opened drawers to assemble the clothes she was going to wear. 'A car stopped and the driver asked me if I'd like a lift.'

'That was decent of him.'

'I . . . I don't think it was. I'm sure he was after me. When I . . .' As she dressed, she told him what happened.

He was of a more phlegmatic character than she and was seldom concerned about what might have happened, but hadn't. 'He didn't make any sort of a move?'

'Didn't have the chance.'

'And you'd no doubts until he yanked the dog away from the window?'

'But he just didn't care that he was hurting the poor little beast,' she answered, as she wriggled a petticoat down over her shoulders.

'Don't you think that it's because that upset you, you became alarmed?'

'It was more than just the way he treated the dog. There seemed to be a funny expression in his eyes . . .' In the bedroom, with husband and dogs by her side, it was easy to judge that her fears had probably been totally groundless and the driver had been doing no more than trying to help. 'I suppose I must have been imagining things,' she said, happy to convince herself that this was so.

CHAPTER 7

Walker-Jones suffered the sour bitterness of frustrated failure. He'd been so near to persuading her into the car. She had been intensely desirable – young but mature, touched by the gamin quality that suggested a bubbling determination to enjoy life. Mentally, she'd have resisted him throughout, which would have made her physical helplessness all the more exciting . . .

As he reached the end of the road and turned right, he decided it was now so late there was little point in continuing to drive around. Only the more determined prostitutes would be on the streets and none of them could offer him the pleasure he desired. In any case, he had no intention of lowering himself to go with such women.

But frustration prevented his accepting the conclusion he had just reached, while imagination spurred him on. His imagination could become a private cinema which showed films so vivid that they became reality and taunted him . . .

The dog whined and he cursed it. He was convinced that if it hadn't yelped, she'd have accepted his offer and climbed into the car. And soon he'd have said that something was catching his foot so he must stop to discover what it was . . .

He drove around a corner and there, well ahead, walking away from him along the left-hand pavement, were two women, obviously young. Two were too many. His proven technique demanded a single victim . . . As he watched, they parted; one turned into the tiny front garden of a house, the other looked back to make certain his car was far enough away, then crossed the road. He slowed. They'd been out together, separating when they reached the home of one; the odds had to be that the second woman's house would be nearby. Would the one disappear into her house before the other reached hers? He daren't slow the car any more or he must attract suspicion . . .

As he drew abreast of the first woman, she opened the front door. In the rear-view mirror, he was able to catch the moment when the light from inside was cut off as the door was closed. The second woman began to veer across the pavement which surely meant she had almost reached her home. He had to act very quickly or not at all. He cut across the road, braked to a halt, leaned over to lower the window. The dog made as if to try to escape and he held on to it, careful not to seem to be using any great force. 'I say,' he called out.

She hesitated.

'Can you help me?' The streetlighting was good enough to show a woman in her late teens, no beauty yet enjoying the attraction of youth, dressed in a mildly patterned raincoat that was still damp, although the rain had stopped.

'What is it?' she asked, her hand on the gate.

'I'm trying to find the London road, but seem to be going round in circles.'

'Carry on to the end of this road, turn right and then second right.'

He cupped his ear. 'What was that?' With his other hand, he squeezed a fold of the dog's belly, making it yelp repeatedly. He leaned back, opened the driving door, stepped out on to the pavement. 'Sorry about the row,' he said. 'Rex is telling the world he should have been fed a long time ago. He would have been if this place didn't have the most complicated system of one-way roads I've ever met.' He smiled. 'My wife's going to laugh at me. She's always said I've no sense of direction.'

She briefly smiled in return.

He'd thought about trying to persuade her into the car, but had decided that that was virtually impossible. He was going to have to overcome her on the pavement and then bundle her into it. On the face of things, potentially very dangerous, but at this time of night, suburbanites were normally either watching television or in bed. He came round

43

the bonnet of the car, his gloved hand in the pocket of his sports jacket.

He advanced until it was obvious that she was beginning to become uneasy. 'Would you be kind enough to tell me again which way to go to reach the London road?'

'Up to the end, turn right, then second right. It's sign-posted.'

'Thanks a lot. Do you have a dog?'

'Mum won't let me because she doesn't like 'em.'

'That really is a pity.' He shuffled his feet to gain a few more inches. Her uneasiness increased until she became alarmed. He tightened his fingers to crush the phial in the pad he held in his coat pocket, brought his hand out and went to force the pad over her nostrils and mouth. She reacted much more quickly than he'd anticipated and she flailed at him, desperately trying to keep him at bay; one hand knocked off his hat. He managed to draw her hard up against himself and as she began to scream, he clapped the pad over her face. Her struggles became more violent and he almost lost hold of her, then they weakened and she suddenly collapsed, only staying upright because of his grasp.

He was sweating, out of breath, and both triumphant and frightened. But there were no angry shouts, no sounds of pounding feet. The road remained empty. He dragged her the few feet to the car, opened the front passenger door. The dog made to jump out and he grabbed it with one hand, careless that he almost lost his grip on her, and hurled it back inside, squealing. To force the woman into the car proved to be much more difficult than expected because one or other of her limbs seemed to gain independent life and move to thwart him as it snagged on something, but in the end he succeeded. He shut the door, collected up his hat.

Once behind the wheel, he found his hands were shaking. He engaged first, drove away from the pavement. The road remained a pool of surburban quiet. He kept well within the speed limit, even though in a hurry to reach the darkness and relative seclusion of the countryside before she regained consciousness. As he drove, he accepted that he had a problem. The streetlighting had been good, she had seen him out of the car, and when she'd knocked his hat off, his face had been fully visible. So unless her memory proved to be permanently scrambled by shock, she'd be able to give the police a much more detailed description of him than had the other women. Were he ever identified as a possible suspect (and he was clever enough to accept that through totally unforeseen circumstances he might be) her evidence could prove fatal to him. How to escape the danger? The question had only to be asked for the answer to be blindingly obvious. He felt as if he'd swallowed hot fire.

CHAPTER 8

Adeane entered the administration-block car park at Lantair Motors and drove towards his bay, only to find a car already in it. He was amused by this breach of office etiquette, not annoyed as many would have been. He backed and drove across to one of the bays for visitors.

He entered his office and hung his mackintosh on the old-fashioned coat stand, puzzled by the thought that something about the room was odd. When he approached his desk and took more careful note of it, he realized what that something was – the top was clear, yet when he'd left just before lunch the previous day, to go up to London on business, he'd set out files and reference books that were germane to work that had to be finished before the end of the week. He sat, lifted the receiver of the internal phone, dialled. 'Anne.'

'Who's that?'

'Who would you like it to be – Hugh Grant?'

'But . . .'

'Who's been at my desk?'

There was no immediate answer.

'Did you clear all the papers that were on it?'

'No.'

'Then who did?'

Another silence.

'Are you still in the land of the living?'

'Hasn't anyone . . . kind of spoken to you?'

'About what?'

The line went dead. Perplexed, he stared at the far wall. Anne's equivocation inevitably suggested she was responsible for moving the papers and was reluctant to admit this for fear of his anger, but in the past, if she'd done anything incorrectly, she'd always been prepared to accept responsibility. He dialled again; another woman answered and said Anne had just left the room. As he replaced the receiver, the door opened and she stepped inside the room. 'I've been trying to get back on to you,' he said. He indicated the top of his desk. 'As bare as a page-three girl. Who's responsible?'

'Didn't Fred . . . ?' She stopped.

'Didn't he what?'

'Give you the message.'

'I came into the building through the back entrance. Have you any idea what message he was meant to give me?'

'To go straight up and see Mr Hesketh.'

'A pleasure delayed is not inevitably a pleasure sharpened. Are you inferring that somehow he is responsible for all my things being moved?'

She fiddled with one of the buttons on her dress. 'Yesterday afternoon, he gave orders for your desk to be cleared.' She hesitated, then added: 'Alison did it because I wouldn't.'

He stared at her, gripped by fear. To escape this, he reacted in typical manner and suggested a motive that was plainly ridiculous. 'At long last the dinosaurs have recognized the worth of PR and I've been promoted to the board floor?'

She shook her head. 'It's so beastly unfair,' she said with passion.

She was fortunate if she'd lived to her age and not discovered that life didn't know the meaning of 'fair'.

'Why can't they be honest, instead of going on about the need to reorganize?'

'Euphemisms, not love, keep the world turning.'

'I hate them!' She turned and left.

He stared through the window at the sky in which a solitary cotton-wool cloud drifted eastwards. At breakfast, Patricia had been in one of her bubbly moods and there had been a moment when he'd stepped back from himself and thought what a lucky man he was. Confucius say, man think happy, man about to step on banana skin.

The banana skin could not be held at bay for ever. He lifted the receiver of the internal phone, dialled. 'I understand you want to see me, Gerry?'

'Yes.'

'Shall I come up now?'

'Yes.' The connection was cut.

Hesketh was a stolid, humourless company man, but he'd always been perfectly pleasant and hadn't pulled rank – until now. It reminded Adeane that when Bartons had made him redundant, many of those who had retained their jobs and with whom he had previously been on friendly terms had suddenly distanced themselves from him. Bad luck was catching.

He drove out of the car park and in the direction of Rander's Road, suddenly slowed and drew into the side, causing the driver of the light van immediately behind to brake sharply and shout angrily. He drummed his fingers on the steering wheel. Return home and it would be to an empty house and there was the guarantee that his black thoughts would become blacker. He needed to do something or talk to someone which or who could lift the clouds sufficiently for him to regain a little hope. A day in London, amongst the crowds? London, like all major cities, offered much to the rich, envious frustration to everyone else. An aimless drive to anaesthetize his mind – surely he'd remain so occupied with his thoughts that it would be his driving that would be anaesthetized? The company of a friend? Did he know anyone whose sense of loyalty to friendship was strong enough to stand his moaning . . . ?

Twenty-one minutes later, he turned into Turnbull Farm and braked to a halt. The house, in full sunshine, was at its most attractive. The moss made patterns on the roof, the chunky central chimney cast a shadow that, because of the edges of the tiles, looked like a cartoonist's dunderheaded politician, the colours of the variegated bricks were clearly defined.

Diana met him at the front door. 'No work?'

'No.'

'Just, no?'

'I need to talk to someone.'

'Why not your friend?'

'She's at the *Gazette*.'

'I believe the telephone has been invented.'

'Someone who'll . . . who'll understand.'

She stared straight at him. 'I'm not certain whether that's complimenting or insulting my intelligence, but until I know for sure, I'll accept the former. Come on in.'

They went into the sitting-room.

'Would you like a drink or is it too early?'

'It's not too early.'

'Gin, whisky, Cinzano, or lager?'

After she had gone out of the room, he crossed to the window. The lawn had been newly cut and the striping ran from side to side rather than from end to end, as it had always done when he'd been doing the mowing. This, ridiculously, angered him. To the extent that when she returned, a glass in each hand, he said: 'Who cut the lawn?'

'Old Man Lawson's nephew. He's doing odd-jobbing gardening to make enough money to buy a motorcycle. Why d'you ask?'

'He's done it the wrong way.'

She put a glass down on the occasional table by one armchair for him, sat.

'It should be mown end to end, not across.'

'That, surely, is no longer for you to decide?'

'Goddamnit, I . . .' He regained control of his common sense. 'Sorry. I'm talking like a bloody idiot.'

'Which is sufficiently unlike you, when you're not making jokes, that it suggests something's very wrong. Settle down and tell me what's happened.'

When he was seated, he said: 'When I arrived at work this morning it was to find my desk had been cleared.'

'What's the significance of that?'

'It's the coward's way of presenting the bad news.'

'Are you saying you've been sacked?'

'In an age when a spade is called an artefact of manual

levitation, I've been made redundant because of re-organization.'

'Why?'

'Remember my telling you how difficult things could be at Lantair's because of office politics?'

'The old fuddy-duddy you replaced has been made a consultant and he has the ear of the chairman?'

'One of the innovations I introduced, naturally to Emms's strongest objections, was visits by foreign journalists. They cost and had Sir Edward moaning. Recently, one of the journalists crashed a top-of-the-line Lantair, which meant a thirty-thousand-pound write-off on top of the normal cost of a visit. Emms couldn't get to Sir Edward quickly enough to point out this was the route to financial ruin and that gave Sir Edward an additional duodenal ulcer. He waited his chance, then called a special meeting of the board, certain he could persuade them of the need for change, since one of the younger members has recently died and another was abroad. The board passed a resolution to the effect that the PRO department in its present form could not be financially justified and therefore there should be a reorganization, with all publicity in future to be carried out by existing departments, advised – naturally – by Emms.'

'Surely the smashed car was a one-off disaster?'

'Of course.'

'Then to say all future visits by foreign journalists will be equally expensive is ridiculous.'

'The right to be ridiculous is one of the most cherished privileges of British management.'

'Can other departments handle the work you've been doing?'

'Do you ask a butcher to remove your appendix?'

'Presumably you can sue for wrongful dismissal?'

'They're doing everything by the book. Even paying me over-the-odds redundancy money.'

'Then at least you have something to fall back on?'

'Yes, but . . .'

'Money doesn't heal pride?'

'I was doing a damned good job. Sales have been on a rising curve.'

'Surely you pointed that out to the chairman?'

'When Gerry gave me my marching orders, I said I wanted to see Sir Edward. He's out of the country.'

'And Gerry can't help?'

'Won't. He thinks what the chairman thinks.'

'Put your case to the full board.'

'Rumour has it that the chairman's taking on two more close pals which will tip the balance permanently in his favour. In any case, while it's simple to show the direct effect of bad publicity, it's very difficult to prove that increased sales are primarily due to good publicity.'

She drained her glass, held it in the palm of her left hand. 'What are the prospects of finding another job?'

'At my age, poor.'

'Ageism is out.'

'Tell that to employers.'

'Surely you'll find someone with the wit to value what you can offer?'

'After being sacked twice in three years, I wonder if I have anything to offer.'

'Are you really that weak and feeble?'

He did not resent her words. He might originally have told himself he sought her sympathy, but in truth it was her fighting spirit he needed.

She stood. 'I'll get refills.'

'You wouldn't rather I left?'

'If I did, I wouldn't be offering you another drink.'

'I'd forgotten how direct you always are.'

'They say that the mind forgets what it doesn't want to remember.' She stepped forward and held out her hand for his glass.

He watched her leave. It was because she was so direct, so reluctant to use politeness or equivocation as camouflage for what she truly thought, that many of their rows had been so bitter.

She returned, handed him his glass, sat. 'Did you know

51

that Tom owns a much bigger company as well as Royal Motors?'

'Can't say I did.'

'Nor did I until I had a meal with Serena at home and she drank considerably more than usual because something had obviously upset her badly – not that she'd say what; became painfully embarrassed when I was curious. Anyway, after the third or fourth postprandial cognac, she started talking about Tom, rather wildly, really. Said he owns this very big company, but keeps that fact a dark secret.'

'Why so – do they manufacture shocking-pink condoms?'

'They're in scrap and specialize in cars.'

'Then why the secrecy? I know Tom's turned snobbism into an art form, but recycling is the buzz word of the age. He could present himself as our saviour; perhaps even with a large S.'

'The business was started by his grandfather who went through the streets with a mule cart, shouting: "Any old iron?"'

'So the old boy started at the bottom of the ladder. Marks and Sparks began as a stall in the market. Tom's so rich and successful now, he could laugh off a grandfather who peppered and salted little children before he ate them.'

'Most people in his position could, he can't.'

'Why not?'

'Because he was so scarred by life when he was young, he tries to hide the past even from himself.'

'Serena managed to work that out? She must have been eating a lot of fish.'

'It's my conclusion after hearing all that happened to him . . . After his grandfather died, his father drank all the profits, beat up his mother, fathered two illegits by a woman who lived in the same road, and ignored him. These by-blows were as hale and hearty as he was weak and feeble and they bullied him in retaliation for their illegitimacy.

'His father died when he was fifteen. He said he was going to carry on the scrap business which had virtually become moribund; people laughed at the idea. But the business was all that his mother had to rely on for an income, so if it failed she'd have to apply for state aid and she saw living on that as the final degradation.

'He turned out to be far more successful than anyone had thought possible. And as the business thrived and expanded over the years, he gave his mother all the luxuries she'd never before enjoyed. Then she was diagnosed as suffering from Alzheimer's. He nursed her through four years of hell, during which she descended into a mindless cabbage; after she died, he suffered a nervous breakdown. Eventually, he managed to pull himself together and return to work. But something in his character had been changed by all his mental suffering. Before, he'd been careful, seldom, if ever, taking risks; after, he seemed almost eager to gamble. Ironically, it all paid off and brought him to where he is now.'

'A satisfying history for all those who idealistically believe that nobility of spirit is rewarded here as well as there. But why exactly have you told me all this?'

'So you can understand that it's not fair to judge him solely on appearances.'

'Does it matter how I judge him?'

'You'll never take the trouble to get on with someone unless you can respect him.'

'You're wanting me to respect Tom?'

'That would help when you ask if he'll give you a job.'

He stared at her in open astonishment. 'If I did that, he'd laugh himself to death.'

'You're not trying to understand, are you? He sees you as someone who couldn't be less like himself, but you're married to me, so you're family. What I've told you shows that for him, family is all-important. He'll find you a job if you can suffer yourself to allow him to.'

'And if he did, d'you know why? Not because I'm family. Because it would give him the pleasure of seeing me kow-tow.'

'God, you men! Pride goeth to the stake with head held high ... When you said earlier you doubted you'd find another job because of your age, you seemed to have had all the stuffing knocked out of you. That made me want to help, even though it's not my job any longer. What a terrible waste of time and effort!'

He finished his drink. Women had never been ready to take the trouble to understand men. 'It seems to be an appropriate time to leave.'

She did not disagree.

CHAPTER 9

Despite perceived wisdom, after retirement Camm felt neither bored nor discarded. Indeed, he enjoyed life more than when he had been working. Even Edna, his wife, could find no reason to complain because he was around the house for much of the time – he was for ever giving her a hand.

He took Hatter – a giant schnauzer – for a walk on most fine mornings. Frequently he went via Steps Woods where he could let Hatter loose for a run, since there was no game and she could disturb only rabbits and squirrels, the chasing of which left her panting and sufficiently tired temporarily to behave with the decorum usual to a five-year-old bitch.

He settled on the trunk of a fallen tree a couple of hundred yards into the wood and lit a cigarette, experiencing a frisson of guilt because Edna never stopped trying to persuade him to give up smoking. The sun was warm and he fell into a reverie, remembering brief snatches from the past that gave amusement or pleasure; the wedding cake for their young daughter that had been shaped like a cricket bat because her husband was a keen player, the time just before his marriage to Edna when they'd viewed the main bedroom of a flat to let and had got the giggles, his second day at work when he'd knocked over a vase of flowers into the toothy typist's lap . . .

Hatter's barking jerked his mind back to the present. Something or someone was disturbing her – an easy thing to do. He came to his feet and walked further into the wood, calling on her to shut up and not be stupid, knowing from experience that both commands were futile. He rounded a solitary, thick clump of rhododendrons to come into a natural clearing and saw Hatter, head pointing straight ahead and slightly down, legs so balanced that if necessary she could run like hell. 'What are you on about?' he demanded. She turned her head, then looked back and resumed barking.

He went forward. Four paces on, beyond a thick clump of brambles, he saw two legs, wide apart, from mid thigh downwards. The legs had the form and smoothness of a woman's. 'Oh, dear!' he said in his mind as he came to a stop. He coughed loudly and repeatedly so that the couple could return to earth and make themselves presentable, failing from embarrassment to realize that if there were a couple there, they must have been alerted by Hatter to the fact that their privacy had been invaded.

The legs did not move. Hatter, emboldened by his presence, moved slowly forward a few paces, came to a stop; her barking changed in character from defensive to offensive. Unwillingly, he realized he might have stumbled on tragedy, not lubricity. Kind hearted, upset by the sight of blood and unnerved by tragedy, his instinct was to hurry out of the wood and leave someone else to determine the facts. But he was old-fashioned and honoured duty, so he went forward.

The young woman was naked; she lay on her back, her arms behind her; she had been blindfolded and gagged with masking tape.

Feeling sick, he turned and ran, followed by Hatter who barked excitedly.

'Where?' asked the detective inspector, phone to the right ear.

'Steps Wood, sir. That's half a mile beyond –'

'I know where it is. Approximate age, height, weight, description?' He listened. 'Is the area taped off?'

'There's only my mate here, but we're doing what we can. It's a fair-sized wood and –'

'I'll have more hands with you as soon as possible. I want the woods blanked off. Have you contacted the owner?'

'No, sir. Thought it best to get in touch with you first.'

He replaced the receiver, stood, walked round his desk and across to the large-scale map of the division that hung on the far wall. Steps Wood was roughly four miles from

Banners Cross. The description just given matched that of Jane Rowland, reported missing very early the previous morning. 'Shit!' he said, his anger momentarily unchecked. Every time a person was reported missing, he hoped that that person would be one of the ninety-nine per cent who later surfaced or could be proved to be unharmed. With two daughters of his own, he knew how he felt when they were only a couple of hours adrift.

He phoned the detective chief superintendent at county HQ and reported the facts. That call concluded, he left his room and went next door to the detective sergeant's. 'It looks like the Rowland woman has turned up dead, in Steps Wood, after being raped.'

'Shit!' exclaimed the DS, unconsciously repeating what the other had said.

'Notify the coroner, doctor, and pathologist; send out as many hands as you can muster, plus SOCOs. Find out who's the owner of the wood and say we'll be blanking it off whilst investigations are carried out. Have we been given a photo of Jane Rowland?'

'Jim said the father had handed one to the officer who had a word with him. I'll get hold of it.'

'As quick as you can.'

The DI drove out of divisional HQ and across town, through country lanes bordered by stone walls to Steps Wood. Although it was relatively lightly inhabited countryside, already a number of onlookers had gathered, drawn there by a macabre interest in a tragedy that would have sickened them if ever they were to come face to face with the reality.

Yellow police tape had been run along the edge of the wood and a constable, in shirt-sleeves, was on watch in the road. The wooden gate, one bar slumped because the wood had rotted, moss growing on it in a couple of places, was swung back. The route along the ride to be followed by everyone was marked by small red flags, set by SOCOs – scene-of-crime officers. Fifty yards in, a plastic yellow number tag had been fixed outside the flagged path. The DI stopped and visually examined the ground by the tag. A rusting bolt lay amongst the sparse grass. There was small chance that this was of any significance, but in a major crime no evidence, however irrelevant it initially appeared to be, was immediately downgraded, as happened in minor crimes when there was never enough time. He continued along the ride to the clearing.

A SOCO was videotaping the general scene, commentating into the microphone as he did so; two more were on hands and knees, searching between lengths of string that had been run out to form a grid that would enable them to ensure no square inch of ground was missed.

He stared down at the body and experienced a familiar, disturbing emotion which was a compound of sadness, anger, embarrassment, and the bitter certainty that man had a much greater capacity for evil than good. Because the police doctor had not yet arrived to pronounce her dead – necessary even though nothing could have been more dreadfully certain – she lay as she had been found. He took from his inner coat pocket the colour snap of a laughing young woman who was enjoying life to the full and compared this with the dead woman who had suffered mental and physical agony before death had rescued her. Despite the fact that much of the lower part of the face was obscured by masking tape, he could be certain she was Jane Rowland.

Later, he was going to have to tell the parents that she was dead; that before she had been murdered, she had almost certainly suffered sexual assaults. This was a task that more often than not was left to junior officers, but he believed command did not afford a man the opportunity to evade a duty, however much he might wish that it did.

CHAPTER 10

Adeane heard the front gate click shut and he went through to the hall as Patricia stepped inside. She closed the front door, faced him. 'Well?'

Her expectant tone alerted him to the fact that he was expected to comment on something. He noticed her dress. 'A new outfit?'

'I saw it when I went out to lunch and simply had to try it on. Couldn't take it off.' She put the green carrier bag, adorned with the image of a large golden crown, which contained the frock she had been wearing, on the hall chair. She twirled, causing the full skirt to swirl. 'Don't you think it's absolutely me?'

Being male, he thought that it had probably cost a lot of money. 'Very much you,' he replied ambiguously.

'The woman in the shop said it suited me so well because I have the perfect figure. She wouldn't believe I've never been a model.'

Obviously very well clued up on feminine psychology, the saleswoman had known exactly how to cause Patricia to throw all thoughts of financial prudence to the four winds.

'Don't you think I look good in it?'

'Very attractive.'

'You don't sound all that enthusiastic.'

'I've a bit of a frog in my throat.'

She moved until she could look at her image in the hall mirror. 'One reason I bought it is, it'll be perfect for the weekend.'

'What's so special about next weekend?'

'Don't you ever listen to anything I tell you? Not next

weekend. The one when we go to France for the day for a special meal.'

'I don't think we'll be able to go.'

'God! Not again? You're as sour as vinegar. Of course we're going.'

'I've had one hell of a day and –'

'D'you think mine's been a bed of roses with that old bitch doing her best to upset me? But didn't I get my own back on her this morning!' She chuckled as she moved one shoulder, then the other. 'I wonder if it needs a slight alteration around the neck? I did suggest this to the woman, but she swore it wasn't necessary. I'm not so certain.'

'There's something you must know.'

'When you've poured me a drink. We must celebrate.'

'Celebrate what, exactly?'

'Are you determined to make life miserable? Celebrate me finding this dress, of course. And maybe a good drink or two will make you less of a hedgehog.' She picked up the carrier bag and crossed to the stairs, climbed them.

He watched her. She was exaggerating the movement of her hips. She was probably on some Parisian catwalk, enjoying the applause of the rich and the famous. He'd not met anyone else so excited by praise; there were times when it was as if she were still a child.

He poured out drinks, carried them through to the sitting-room to find she was not yet down. He was unsurprised. She would be in front of the full-length mirror in the bathroom, admiring herself. Diana, whilst never careless about her appearance, could never be bothered to primp . . . He pulled his thoughts up to a sharp stop. Such comparisons were not only meaningless, they were dangerous.

Eventually she returned downstairs, now wearing casual clothes. He handed her a glass. 'I'm afraid we've got to face up to something. We can't go to France for a meal.'

'Why not?' she demanded as she sat.

'Because of the cost.'

'You and money! You can't think of anything else, like some beastly miser. Maybe that's what you really are.'

'It would help if you'd think about it a little more often.'

'What's that supposed to mean?'

'The dress you've just bought must have cost –'

'Paid for with my own money. Are you now going to try to tell me I can't spend that how I like?'

'There are times when one has to hold back.'

'Well, I'm not holding back. And if you're so bloody mean you won't go to France, stay here.'

'I'm asking you not to go.'

'And I'm telling you, I will go.'

'We have to watch the pennies . . .'

'You watch 'em. I've better things to do.'

He said harshly: 'I got the push this morning.'

She stared at him, puzzled.

'When I arrived at work, I had the message to see Gerry. He told me that the board's decided to close down the PR department, which makes me redundant. As from this morning, I'm out of a job.'

'Oh, my God! What are we going to live on?'

'I'll be receiving some redundancy money.'

'How much?'

'I won't know that for a few days; Accounts have to work things out. But since they said they'll be paying me more than is legally due, it should come to a few thousand.'

'Then we can go to France.'

'You're not understanding. The redundancy money plus the little the state pays the unemployed will be all I have. I've no capital.'

'And you know why? Because of your wife.'

'That's not fair.'

'If you hadn't kept paying her most of what you earn, you'd have the capital to make certain we don't have to live like beggars.'

'I wouldn't call it living like beggars just because we can't go to France with Fred and Caroline for a meal.'

'Didn't you hear me? I'm going.'

'I was hoping you'd realize that we need to pool the money and go very carefully until I find another job.'

'You expect me to keep you?'

'To help meet the running costs.'

She drained her glass. 'I want another drink,' she said aggressively, challenging him to deny it on the grounds of economy.

As he stood, he reflected that she had not said how sorry she was that he should have been made redundant.

For him, sex could be solace as well as pleasure; it could wash away bitterness and suggest a sunny future. Diana had understood this and responded, even when she would have preferred not to; Patricia, who seldom considered others, neither understood, nor would she have responded even if she had. So, he'd told himself earlier, whatever his feelings, it was going to be a night of unruffled sheets.

Decisions, he decided, as she undressed slowly and then carefully studied her body in the mirror, could be easy to make, but difficult to accept. 'Come to bed,' he said, his voice slightly hoarse.

She did not immediately make any response, but continued to move and study herself from different angles. Then she crossed to the bed, leaned over to bring out her nightdress from under the right-hand pillows.

'Don't put that on.'

She slipped the nightdress over her head. 'I've a terrible headache,' she said, as she climbed into bed.

Every woman's lifeline.

It was only after the lights were out and he was finding it difficult to fall asleep that it occurred to him that when she'd been standing in front of the mirror and moving around as revealingly as possible, she had been deliberately provoking him in order to deny him his pleasure because he was trying to deny her hers.

CHAPTER 11

Because of the seriousness of the crime, the postmortem on Jane Rowland was carried out on Saturday afternoon. The pathologist, recording through an overhead microphone every move he made and every judgement he reached, worked quickly and efficiently, helped by his assistant. Also present were a forensic scientist who bagged specimens and handed them on to the uniform PC who recorded and logged all relevant details, a SOCO, and the DI who had not become inured to the sights and sounds, despite the many years he had been subjected to them – he tried to sustain an intelligent interest while picturing sunny days on the water in a friend's small yacht.

The pathologist removed disposable apron and gloves, washed with medical soap. He dried his hands, then said to the DI: 'Shall we go outside?' He led the way out on to the small front lawn – the mortuary was built to resemble as closely as possible a suburban bungalow in order to help people ignore the reality. He brought an old-fashioned cigarette case from his pocket and offered it.

'No, thanks.'

'Scared of calling on my services?' The pathologist, a small, sharply featured man who looked and dressed like the abstemious intellectual he was not, opened the case and extracted a cigarette. He lit this, inhaled with evident pleasure, his head tilted upwards to enjoy the warmth of the sun. 'She was in good physical condition and her death was due to strangulation. This was carried out by the two thumbs exerting pressure on the windpipe. Almost certainly, the murderer sat astride her body as he strangled her.

'She was raped, probably more than once, and suffered

further sexual assaults. No sperm was deposited which means the murderer was wearing a condom of extra strength or, in turn, several of ordinary strength.

'There were no foreign traces on her body. Since it's normal for there to be at least an exchange of one or more pubic hairs during sexual activity, we have the same MO as reported previously – a very thorough search of the victim's body after the assaults have been concluded.

'On opening the lungs, there was the possible scent of chloroform, but so faint that although I have no doubt it was used, I will not be able to swear this was so in the witness-box.

'And that's about it. You'll have the written report just as soon as my secretary can prepare it.' He drew on the cigarette, dropped the stub to the ground. 'He's smart. Most men driven by an overwhelming sexual urge do not pay attention to detail; he has the wit to understand what incriminating traces a rapist usually leaves, plans how to avoid leaving any of these, executes his plan.'

'If we identify a suspect, you won't be able to provide enough evidence to ensure a conviction?'

'I'm afraid that's the strength of it. Your hope must be that the necessary evidence comes from another source.'

The DI scuffed the toe of his shoe across the grass. 'I've been on to the other forces and they've sent me the evidence from the rapes. It doesn't help, and the facts in this case aren't taking us anywhere, so we have to face the possibility that we're not going to get any further . . . He hasn't killed before. Why this time? The obvious answer is that he judged it necessary. The pick-up wasn't as clean as usual and she had too good a look at him before he rendered her unconscious and then blindfolded her. What effect is the murder going to have on him?'

'You're asking if it might turn him from a rapist into a rapist and murderer? I'm no psychiatrist, Inspector, but from my work I've gained the impression that a man who finds pleasure in perversity can eventually only maintain that level of pleasure by increasing the degree of his perversity.'

'Then I hope to God we strike lucky very quickly.'

*   *   *

64

The DC led the way to No. 56, knocked. The front door was opened by a middle-aged, dumpy woman who wore large, wide-rimmed glasses that did nothing for her appearance.

'Mrs Potter?'

She nodded.

'My name's Detective Constable Penfold and this is WPC Connor. Sorry to bother you like this, but we'd very much like a word with your daughter.'

'Liz is terribly upset,' she replied uncertainly.

'Of course she is, but we really do need to talk to her,' said the WPC.

'But in her state . . . I don't know.'

'It is very, very important.'

'I suppose you'd best come in, then.' She showed them into the front room, said uneasily: 'I've not had time to tidy up.'

'Don't you worry. And I don't mind admitting, it's a lot tidier than my sitting-room.'

Mrs Potter left, closing the door behind herself. The DC picked up a newspaper that had been on the arm of the settee and skimmed the front page, the WPC studied a print that hung on the wall behind the television.

The door opened and Liz entered, then nervously came to a halt just inside. Grief had thickened and coarsened her features, shock had dulled her so that initially she seemed to be of limited intelligence.

The WPC spoke with friendly warmth. 'Hullo, Liz. I'm Stella and this is Brian. He comes from Exeter, but that's not really his fault. Why not sit down and get comfortable?'

The girl moved to the settee, sat, clasped her hands in her lap.

'We wouldn't be bothering you at such a terribly sad time, only you maybe can help us a lot.'

She stared into the past and her eyes began to water.

'You must be brave. Jane would want you to be, wouldn't she?'

After a moment, she nodded.

'We're going to find out who did this terrible thing and you're going to help us do that.'

'I didn't see nothing,' she said, her voice choked. 'I said good night, see you in the morning. That's all. I mean, she only had to cross the road to her place. If I'd of known . . . If I'd waited until she was in her house . . .' She swallowed heavily.

'You couldn't have known and you'd no reason to suspect anything was going to happen, so there's nothing for you to blame yourself for. You must understand that.'

'But . . .'

'There can only be blame if someone knows, but doesn't act . . . Now, help us all you can. Tell us what happened, starting with the two of you going to the disco.'

At first she spoke haltingly, but soon with greater fluency, seemingly gaining some relief from talking. At the disco, they'd met two boys they knew and had danced with them, but had refused to stay on; they'd caught the bus back. They'd left the bus at the top of the road and walked along the pavement. One or two cars had passed them, then a very noisy motorcycle. When they'd reached her house, they'd said a brief good night. It hadn't begun to occur to her to watch to make certain Jane reached home safely; they'd parted like that times beyond counting and nothing had happened. Yet if only she'd not gone indoors until she'd watched to make certain Jane had reached her home safely . . .

'Like I said, you mustn't blame yourself, because there was no reason for you to have worried,' said the WPC, managing not to sound in the least impatient. 'Are you sure there was no one else walking along the pavement on either side of the road?'

She was certain. Then she wasn't so certain. There'd been no one near them, but there might just have been someone further away whom she hadn't noticed.

'And what about cars?'

'Only the old banger what had turned in from Naders Crescent.'

'Had that passed by the time you came indoors?'

She thought for a moment. 'I don't remember. Maybe not since it was going so slowly.'

'How do you know that?' the DC asked.

The question, and the sharpness with which it had been put, confused her. 'Well, I . . . I don't rightly know.'

'It was an impression and probably quite right,' said the WPC, giving her companion a quick look of reproof. 'You think it was an old car?'

'A Morris Oxford?'

'You know your cars, then?'

'A boyfriend had one. Always breaking down. Genuine, that is. But he was ever so proud of it.' For a very brief while, she enjoyed a memory.

The DI rubbed his forehead, trying to ease the thumping pain. As he grew older, he was discovering that unusual stress so often provoked a headache, to the worry of his wife. 'She's certain?'

DC Penfold, who stood in front of the desk, said: 'Yes, guv.'

'But production of them was stopped years ago. I doubt there's more than a handful left on the roads.'

'Does sound a bit unlikely, but she had a boyfriend with one.'

'She's not come up with anything to suggest this car had anything to do with the murder?'

'Only that it was going very slowly. The driver reckoned one of 'em would soon be out of sight indoors and didn't want to be too near the other until that happened.'

'Pure supposition.'

'Not much else to go on, is there?'

'Bugger all.'

Penfold left the room. The DI fiddled with a pencil. If one were setting out in a car to pick up a woman in order to rape her, one surely would want to be as certain as was possible that the car would not break down. Broadly speaking, the older the car, the more likely it might break down. So would a rapist drive a car the production of which had ceased years before; more especially when its age might cause attention to be drawn to it? The obvious answer was, he was either too stupid or too blinded by his perverted urge to realize the increased risk he would then run. Yet as the pathologist had earlier made clear, the lack of evidence pointed to the fact that the rapist was a man clever enough to foresee all possible dangers and sufficiently in command of himself to take successful steps to avoid them. So if he had been driving a Morris Oxford, his reason for doing so had not been the obvious one. Then what in the hell could it have been?

CHAPTER 12

Adeane reached the crown of the hill and drove into the small viewing point. Since there was only one other car present, he was able to park against the wooden rails and to remain seated as he enjoyed the panoramic view. To the south-east, the sea was just visible as a thin streak of silver; to the west, hills created the horizon; to the north, the wooded land – foreshortening made it appear to be far more heavily wooded than was the case – stretched into an indeterminate distance; Amersford, some four miles away, was an irregular-shaped clutter of indistinct forms, their modern ugliness concealed . . . Pride buttered no parsnips. Tom might, as Diana believed, be prepared to offer him a job because he was (still) the husband of his sister-in-law. All that was certain right now was that once he had another job, Patricia and he would regain the exciting relationship they had enjoyed until recently . . .

In the past, her moods had been black creatures of brief existence, possibly because she could never concentrate on anything for long, and he'd always been able to coax her out of them sooner rather than later. But this latest one had now lasted for four days and rather than dissolving, it had deepened. The previous night, she had provoked a bitter row which had only ended when she'd flounced out of their bedroom to sleep in the spare one. It was, of course, fear and jealousy that provoked her – a fear of hardship that had been exacerbated by an article in *The Times* which had recorded the fact that men over forty were experiencing an ever-growing difficulty in obtaining fresh jobs after being made redundant, a jealousy intensified by Caroline's latest phone call in which she'd talked at length about the forthcoming trip to France that Fred was now suggesting should last not a day, but a week . . .

It was all too easy to recall the bitter rows between Diana and himself which had led to his affair with Patricia and the separation. The latest rows with Patricia had been almost as bitter – if they continued, could their relationship hope to survive, remembering that it rested on a more fragile base and she was not restrained by a sense of responsible loyalty? He didn't think so, which was why he was going to have to swallow his instincts and ask Tom for a job.

He turned off the road and into the quarter-mile-long drive that was lined by ancient, massively impressive oaks. Farthingstone House gradually came into view as the gap of visibility between the two rows of trees widened. It was a very large house, part Carolean, part Georgian, part Victorian; two years previously, a notable architect who worshipped classical standards had, much to Walker-Jones's fury, written an article in which he'd referred to it as an architectural hotchpotch of mistaken form. For Adeane, it was the many quirks of form which gave it so much more character than had it been symmetrically perfect.

He parked by the side of the raised flowerbed in the centre of the turning circle. The last time he'd visited there, which had been with Diana, she had said: 'How this place cries out for a Squire Allworthy, not a man who winces if he gets dung on his shoes.' Walker-Jones only lived there because he believed the ownership of a country estate bestowed great social merit.

He crossed to the noble, or grandiloquent, depending on one's viewpoint, portico. He ignored the massive wrought-iron knocker and pressed the electric bell, set in the stonework to the side.

Pablo – unconsciously parodying the traditional English butler – opened the door, inclined his head, fleetingly smiled a welcome, said: 'Good night, señor, sir.'

'Good evening. Is Mr Walker-Jones in?'

'Only Señora Walky-Hones.' Despite all the tuition to

which he was subjected, he still frequently mangled the name. 'You come, please.'

Adeane followed through the great hall, past knights in armour, geometric patterns of weapons, stags' heads of many points, mounted horns from Africa, a fifty-six-pound salmon in a glass case, and two huge, dreary paintings of hunting scenes, all bought from the previous owner who had preferred money to the memories of past generations.

They went down a wide passage to the Regent's Room – the Prince Regent was said to have taken hot chocolate and rum there one November morning, a tradition scorned by most historians.

'Señor Adeane,' said Pablo, almost getting his pronunciation correct.

'What a wonderful surprise!' Serena said, as she put down the magazine she had been reading.

'Surprise, certainly; wonderful, just maybe.' Adeane went round the highly carved Balinese table, leaned down and kissed her lightly on one cheek.

'Don't be so silly! I'm thrilled to see you after so long a time. Sit down and tell me all your news, but first, what will you drink?'

'A gin and tonic, if I may.'

As she gave the order to Pablo, Adeane settled on one of the leather-covered armchairs. When it came to perfect hostesses, she was top of the class. She'd sounded as if she really were thrilled to see him.

'Now tell me, Richard, how is life with you?' she asked, as Pablo left.

'Like the curate's egg.'

'I'm sure there are many more good parts than bad.'

'I wish I could share your certainty.'

'You know, you haven't changed a bit.'

'Should I apologize?'

'Whatever makes you ask that?'

'The consensus of current opinion seems to be that if I changed, it could only be for the better.'

'I like you just as you are.'

'For that, I am your devoted slave.'

'Really?'

'Provided I'm paid union rates.'

She laughed. 'Have you seen Amelia recently?'

'A few days ago.'

'She's such fun.'

'I'm glad you like her.'

'I've suggested she comes and stays with us for a weekend, or longer. Thomas is thinking of taking up riding and if he does, he'll keep a few horses. She'd love to ride, wouldn't she?'

He remembered Diana's comments about the projected visit. 'I'm not all that sure. She's rather scared of horses.'

'For heaven's sake, why?'

'For no reason that we can think of, but children often develop fears for no readily discernible reason, don't they? Diana said you used to be absolutely terrified of spiders.'

'She's exaggerating.' Serena spoke with sharp annoyance. 'It's just that I didn't like them.'

'Even so, you'll understand.'

Pablo returned with two cut-crystal glasses on a silver salver. He handed out the glasses, left.

She'd read that it was plebeian to say 'Cheers', so said nothing and drank.

'D'you expect Tom to be back soon?' Adeane asked.

'I expected him before now. He's been in Whitchester for a few days and was leaving after lunch. I suggested he went by train to avoid the traffic, but he wouldn't because it meant changing twice and the services have become so terrible. Do you want to see him?'

'Just to have a quick word.'

'Then you didn't come here to see me?'

'On the contrary, it was for the pleasure of your company and only incidentally to talk to him.'

'You're not a very good liar.'

'So I've been told before.'

'You can lie as often as you like when you're being nice and I'll believe you.'

'I'll remember that.' He drained his glass. 'I suppose I ought to be on my way.'

'Now, I don't believe you. You're bored by the company.'

'The company sparkles. It's just that I'm due home.'

'Then had Thomas been here, you wouldn't have been able to talk to him for very long, would you?'

He remained silent.

'No answer? I've always thought of you as someone who's never without one.'

Her manner was arch, as it often was. Soon after Amelia had been born and they'd spent the day at Farthingstone, showing her off, he'd said to Diana that he thought Serena had been flirting with him. Diana had laughed, then said: 'You flatter yourself you're that irresistible? The only man my sister finds truly attractive is one whose bank balance is a telephone number. All she was aiming to do – and succeeded – was to persuade you that she's not the bitch she is.'

The cordless phone on the table by Serena's side rang. She switched it on. 'Yes, darling . . . Of course I've been worried . . . All right, I'll tell them to delay the meal . . . Richard's here . . . Brother-in-law Richard. He wants a word with you . . . No, I've no idea . . . Hurry back safely, sweet.' She switched off, replaced the phone on the table. 'He left late and the traffic's impossible so he'll be another hour. You can stay and have dinner with us and chat with him afterwards.'

'I'm afraid not.'

'I simply won't take no for an answer.'

'Just for once, I'm afraid you'll have to. My supper will be waiting and if I don't turn up to eat it, I'll be in the dog house.'

'I was forgetting that you're not on your own.'

Like hell she had!

'But at least you've time for another drink.'

'Not really.' He stood. 'Many thanks.'

'Now you've remembered where we live, you must visit us more often. You know we always love to see you. But come to think about it, you'll soon be back to talk to Thomas, won't you?'

'As I said, it's not important.'

'Does that mean you won't even bother to come and see me?'

'Like MacArthur, I shall return.' He crossed to kiss her on the cheek.

'Ring for Pablo to show you out.'

'I can manage on my own. Or are you afraid I'll pinch a piece of silver on the way?'

'Can't you think of anything more interesting to pinch?'

He left. The sun was low, forcing him to drop the sun blind of the car. He started the engine, engaged first gear, went round the flowerbed and up the drive. Scuttling away, tail between his legs, he derisively told himself. The odds were that Patricia was not yet home; even if she were, she would not have prepared supper. His only reason for refusing the invitation to dinner had been battered pride. He'd grabbed the chance to leave without having shamefacedly to ask a large favour from a man he disliked and whose attitudes he despised.

CHAPTER 13

'I'm beginning to feel an awful fool,' Pamela Turner said, as she tucked her arm around her husband's.

'Why so?' he asked, as they walked towards the entrance of the council car park.

'Because I'm becoming more and more convinced I was suffering from things that go swish-swoosh in the night.'

'Do what?'

She withdrew her arm so that they could pass single file through the small pedestrian space between the pay booth and the traffic arm, controlled from inside. 'Didn't you frighten everyone sick in the dormitory, including yourself, when after lights out you told your story about the bogles and the beasties that go swish-swoosh in the night?' She linked her arm with his once more as they reached the pavement.

'You're forgetting that I didn't go to boarding school.'

'And how that shows!'

'For the better . . . Look, maybe you were imagining things, but then again, maybe you weren't. We're only a dozen miles from Banners Cross and it did happen on the same night.'

'Yes, I know, but . . .'

'You've more buts than a nanny goat. The police aren't going to die laughing; they're going to listen carefully and then thank you very much for telling them.'

'How do you know that?'

'It's what they're paid to do.'

'You're a great help for my morale, I don't think. Now it won't matter how polite and interested they seem, I'll be certain that in their minds they're calling me a hysterical female.'

'They certainly won't – just so long, of course, as you don't start talking about swish-swooshes.'

She pulled her arm free. 'There are times when it would be a pleasure to push you under a bus.'

They crossed the road, passed through a broad gateway and went up the gently inclined roadway that brought them to the main entrance of the nine-storey, brick-and-glass divisional HQ.

The duty PC in the front room moved down the counter to speak to them. Pamela looked at her husband, he said they'd like a word with someone about something that had happened the previous week. What kind of something? Well, it might just be connected with the horrible murder . . .

'Just a minute, please.' The PC went into the room behind the counter. When he returned, he asked them to wait. They moved across to the small area in which were two tables, with a few tattered magazines on them, and several chairs.

They'd been waiting for little more than three minutes when one of the three doors opened and a middle-aged, noticeably bald man came through; an arm signal from the duty PC directed him to where they sat. 'Mr and Mrs Turner. I'm Detective Constable Wright. If you'd like to come through, we can have a chat.'

They followed him through the doorway, down one narrow corridor and halfway along another, and into a small, square room, painted in two shades of green, whose only furnishings were a wooden table, on which stood recording equipment, four chairs and a framed list of prisoners' rights.

Once they were seated, the DC put a notebook and pencil down on the table. 'I understand you have information concerning the death of Jane Rowland?' His manner was impeccably neutral and gave no hint of the fact that in the past week he, and others, had repeatedly said the same thing, only to find the information given to be useless.

'I'm not sure,' she said, even more uncertain than before.

The DC sighed an internal sigh. 'Tell me what you know, Mrs Turner, and we'll be able to decide.'

'Maybe I was scaring myself. But when he grabbed the

dog so roughly . . . I've always been a dog lover and we have two at home and I'd have more if my husband . . .'

'No offence, but if we start at the beginning and take things as they happened, it'll be much easier for me. Now, what day are we talking about?'

'Last Wednesday.'

'But you waited until today to come here?'

She mentally squared her shoulders. 'I convinced myself I was imagining things and it would just be stupid to say anything. But yesterday there was a talk on the radio about sex crimes and one of the speakers said that an attacker would often use a small friendly dog to give the impression of trustworthiness. When I mentioned that to my husband after he got home from work, he said I must come and tell you that the man in the car had a small dog, which seemed to be trying to get away from him. And no proper dog owner would ever use such unnecessary force . . .'

'Hang on, we're getting ahead of ourselves again. What time are we talking about and where exactly were you?'

Reassured by his friendly manner – and carefully not wondering what he was thinking – she described what had happened that night.

As soon as she finished speaking, Turner, his tone worried, said: 'Could it have been the rapist?'

'Impossible to answer at this stage. Which is why I'm going to ask your wife to return here at a time that best suits her so we can use the computer to create a likeness of the man in the car.'

'I'm afraid I won't be much use at doing that,' she said quickly. 'As I've told you, he was wearing a wide-brimmed hat and that, together with his moustache, meant that much of his face was hidden.'

'You'll most likely do quite a bit better than you think; and in any case, certain features of a face can be almost as useful as the whole face when it comes to identification. The shape of the nose, for instance – you'd be surprised how individual a nose is. And there's another thing, using the computer we can take the best image you can provide and then expunge the moustache and hat and come up with a possible full-face likeness.'

'It sounds as if you think it probably was the rapist,' said Turner.

'Not so. As I mentioned earlier, it's just that we like to follow every lead as far as is necessary.'

'Then at least it's possible it was he?'

Turner was suffering from what was sometimes called post-trauma fear, the DC judged; fear – frequently increased, not diminished, by time – which came from repeatedly worrying about what might have been. 'Right now, many things are possible . . . One last question. Mrs Turner, how sure are you that he was left-handed?'

'Well, I . . . I was quite certain.'

'Are you saying that now you're not?'

'When you ask like that, it makes me think you reckon I could be wrong . . . I don't suppose you can follow that?'

'Easily. But I've absolutely no reason to believe you could be wrong; I was merely trying to evaluate your evidence. You see, if he was the rapist, your evidence about his being left-handed becomes very important.'

She thought back. She said slowly: 'He leaned across the passenger seat and wound the window down to about half-way with his left hand. The dog appeared between him and the windscreen, so it was on his right. He – the dog – scrabbled with his forefeet, trying, I'm quite certain, to find a way of jumping out and escaping. He grabbed the dog very brutally with his left hand . . . I suppose I've been assuming that if he were right-handed, he'd have used his right hand on both occasions, since there was no reason I could see for not doing so.'

He wrote, closed his notebook. 'Thanks very much for telling us about this. We'll be in touch to see when it's most convenient for you to come along and play with our computer.'

The phone rang. Adeane went into the hall and lifted the receiver. 'Three-seven-one-five-six.'

'I called you at work, but you weren't there.'

It was, he thought, typical of Walker-Jones not to bother to identify himself; he assumed people would instantly recognize his voice. ' 'Morning, Tom. How are you?'

'I understand you visited us last night and wanted to speak to me?'

'That's right. Unfortunately, I couldn't wait.'

'The police are incapable of keeping traffic moving. What is the problem?'

'It's not really something that can be discussed over the phone.'

'Is it important?'

His inclination was to say that the matter was totally unimportant so that it could be brushed aside and forgotten, but his conscience refused to allow him to be a coward. 'It is rather, yes.'

'Very well. The day after tomorrow in my office at midday.' He cut the connection.

Adeane replaced the receiver, wondering why so many of the rich thought that curt rudeness was an admirable quality.

In the conference room at county H Q, the assistant chief constable (crime), the detective chief superintendent, and the divisional detective inspector, sat around one end of the large table.

The A C C spoke to the detective chief superintendent. 'Do we have a psychiatrist's opinion?'

'Yes, sir. And like always, it hedges the bets so much one can virtually draw whatever conclusion one wants to. If the four rapes have been committed by the same man, then the diminishing intervals between them may point to someone who is driven by an ever-increasing urge; on the other hand, they might be no more than an indication of opportunity windows.

'Since satisfaction is gained both mentally and physically and since the attainment of the same degree of satisfaction often demands an ever-increasing input of sensation, the killing of the fourth victim may indicate that the rapist now mentally needs to murder as well as rape. On the other hand – once again, the blindingly obvious! – he may have murdered from the purely practical motive of guarding his own safety. However, in this latter case, although he may not have set out with the intention of murdering, having murdered he may have experienced extra pleasure which will have the effect of heightening his future demands.'

'Then surely the odds are that it's probable he'll kill his next victim?'

'It looks like that.'

The ACC briefly drummed on the table with the fingers of his right hand. 'Exactly what do we know about the murderer?'

The detective chief superintendent looked down at the opened folder in front of him. 'The various witnesses' evidence doesn't really take us very far, sir. He's of average size and slightly overweight – I think we need to remember that these are judgements reached only from seeing him inside the car. He's middle aged and suffers from a very slight speech defect which is something less than a lisp – the witnesses agree on this, but find it very difficult to describe. He's probably left-handed. The women who have been raped live in Treighley, Greencastle, and Bledstone; Jane Rowland lived in Banners Cross. This means the rapist either travels extensively throughout the country because of a job or he chooses a totally different area each time in the belief – tragically, accurate – that potential victims will be off their guard. In the Eve Ritchie case, the dog was possibly stolen in Kington.

'We've possible evidence on his car or cars. In the first case, a witness may have seen the victim getting into a car, the date letter of which makes it twelve years old.'

'Sounds unlikely. Why would a man intending rape, knowing his safety depends on a quick getaway, choose a car so old it's potentially unreliable?'

'That would suggest the victim got it wrong, sir, except that in a way it agrees with Liz Potter's evidence. She said good night to Jane Rowland, but just before she went indoors she noticed a car coming down the road very slowly. She identifies it as a Morris Oxford.'

'Production of those ceased years ago.'

'Back in the seventies,' said the DI, speaking for the first time. 'Which is why I've spoken to Liz several times. But she's positive. In my opinion, we should accept that the car was an Oxford. Of course, there's nothing to connect it with the murder other than that it was around at the relevant time and it was being driven slowly. Which might well be because that's all it could do.'

'Do you reckon that's the answer?'

The DI hesitated. 'No, sir. I think it was being driven by the murderer and he was waiting for Liz to go indoors, but I've not an atom of proof to back that up.'

'Accept you're right and we're back to the question I put earlier. Why would the rapist be driving an old banger?'

'At the moment, sir, I've no idea.'

'At least that's an honest answer!' He turned to the detective chief superintendent. 'What about the computer portrait?'

'We hope to have that within the next twenty-four hours, sir.'

'Anything more?'

'Nothing of any relevance.'

The ACC began to drum on the table once more. 'The psychiatrist's report makes it possible we're faced by a man who will not only continue to rape, but murder as well. Normally, this would be cause to issue a warning to women in a specific area to take greater care than usual and any subsequent suggestion of panic could be contained. But here we can't delimit an area, we have to consider the whole country; God knows how people would react. I shouldn't need to remind you that for the past months, both the government and opposition have been using law, order, and the police, as a football in their childish games in parliament. Should we trigger a national panic, the opposition would have a ball at the government's expense, the government would raise hell with us. And one result of that could be the county forces would fail to get the increased funding in the coming financial year that we all so desperately need. Yet it will be even more dangerous to appear to be doing nothing. So we have to be seen to be taking action, but this mustn't be so specific as to cause panic ... I propose we publish details of all we know and appeal to the public for their full cooperation. If they think they're helping, they'll be less inclined to worry.'

'*All* details?' said the DI, his astonishment obvious.

'Yes.'

'But if we do that . . .' He came to a stop.

'I want to hear what you have to say, Inspector.'

'It could give the murderer an idea of how little in fact we know about him.'

'That must be pretty obvious since we're not even questioning anyone.'

'And when we do nail him, we could be left without any jokers to pull out of the hat when we interrogate him.'

'Agreed. But we have to weigh the advantages against the disadvantages. We cover ourselves against the politicians; we engage the public's help – in this sort of case, if they're given the chance they'll always give that a hundred per cent – and provide them with information which may trigger a question in someone's mind, a question that wouldn't otherwise have arisen, and he or she may get in touch with us and provide a lead.' The ACC looked to his right. 'Bob?'

The detective chief superintendent, who never brown-nosed his superiors, yet preferred not to disagree with them too flatly, said slowly: 'All said and done, sir, I tend to be with George. One needs a joker or two up the sleeve, to smack down the clever mouthpiece.'

'One has to match one's wishes to the circumstances. In my opinion, we're in a damned-if-we-do, damned-if-we-don't situation and the only way out of that is what I've just proposed. But if either of you has a better idea, I'd be very glad to hear it.'

There was silence.

'Very well. I'll see the chief constable and clear the proposal with him. Of course, we'll be liaising with the other forces concerned.'

CHAPTER 14

Walker-Jones had opened the showrooms in a prime site in Amersford against all advice, but then he hadn't been concerned about the size of the market for Rolls Royces, Bentleys, Mercedes, and Aston Martins; it was the cachet of representing the marques that he had sought. The world being what it was, since he had not needed the business to be successful, it turned out – when economic times were reasonable – to be highly successful. There was more wealth in the area than most imagined.

Adeane, having had to park some way away, walked up to the imposing doorway of the showrooms. The doorman, in Ruritanian uniform, opened the door for him. The nearer salesman, correctly judging him not to be a prospective customer, took his time about crossing the carpeted floor. 'Yes?'

'I've an appointment to see Mr Walker-Jones.'

'I'll ascertain whether he is free to see you.'

As he waited, Adeane studied an Aston Martin Vantage. A lover of fine cars, it filled him with envious longing, assuaged only by the thought that if he didn't own one, he didn't have to pay the insurance on it.

The salesman returned and directed him upstairs. A middle-aged woman, who sat behind a desk on which was a PC, smiled, thereby dispelling the sternness which her face held when in repose. 'Good morning, Mr Adeane. Mr Walker-Jones is expecting you.' She stood.

He followed her into the large office. Hollywood surely was the inspiration, he thought, as he crossed the deep pile carpet to the antique partners desk on which stood a detailed model in silver of a Ghost. ''Morning, Tom.' On the wall was a large painting of Walker-Jones, looking impressively serious, standing in a Napoleonesque attitude in front of a Bentley Continental.

Walker-Jones nodded his good morning. 'Have a seat.'

Adeane sat on the chair set in front of the desk. He was suddenly reminded of the day – he'd been about twelve – when he'd been summoned to the headmaster's study to explain what, if anything, he knew about the broken window. It was not a memory to bolster his confidence.

'You want a word?'

Tom, he decided, looked like a man who had been put together in a hurry from spare parts. A stranger to harmonious proportions, even the lines on his face were markedly different on the two sides. 'Thanks for finding the time.'

'Happy to help, if I can. But I am rather rushed for time, so if you could come to the point right away?'

'I was wondering . . . Diana suggested . . .' Images of begging bowls floated through Adeane's mind. 'There have been changes at Lantair recently.'

'I thought change was anathema to the company?'

'When it comes to the finished product, that's right.'

'In this country, nostalgia is a highly profitable commodity. Sir Edward is an astute man. You must consider yourself very fortunate to be working for them when so many companies are going to the wall because of trading conditions.'

'As a matter of fact . . .'

'The manager of our other branch needs an assistant salesman and recently advertised for one. He tells me he has had over a hundred applicants, many with good academic qualifications as well as considerable experience. The situation is, of course, worse than the government will allow.'

'The reason I'm here is . . .'

'Can you tell me why all governments lie?'

'Because they're composed of politicians.'

Walker-Jones ostensibly opened a folder on his desk. 'Very nice to have had a word with you after rather a long time. As Serena said this morning, it's a great shame you and Diana have parted, but that's really no reason for not seeing you. She also said you'd be ringing to fix a date for dinner. Make it soon, won't you? . . . Sorry to rush you, but I am very busy.'

'If I could just ask you something?'

He looked at his watch, shut the folder.

'There's been a reorganization of Administration at Lantair. The PR department as it was constituted is being closed down on the grounds of cost, even though increased profits far exceed those costs. That means I've been made redundant.' He waited for comment; there was none. 'So I'm looking for a job. But as you pointed out a moment ago, things are a lot tougher than is generally acknowledged, especially when one's over forty.'

'But surely you aren't that?'

'By a whisker . . . So the future's suddenly turned very sour for me. I make myself responsible for Melly and I've my own place to run, which means expenses are high.'

'Unfortunately, expenses are high for everyone.'

'And out of reach if one isn't earning anything.'

'I confess to being a great believer in the old-fashioned saying that one should cut one's coat according to one's cloth.'

'One needs the cloth to begin with.'

'Presumably, you receive redundancy pay?'

'What I'm statutorily entitled to, plus a little. Since I've only been with Lantair for roughly three years, it's not going to last very long.'

'Then you must hope you will quickly find another job.'

'The outlook is grim enough to make that doubtful. Which is why I was hoping . . .' Adeane came to a stop.

'Well?'

He spoke with a rush. 'Hoping you could help me with a job.'

'I see. If my memory serves me correctly, you were made redundant at your previous job?'

'Yes.'

'Unfortunate.'

'Bartons were taken over and within a year the new company got rid of over half the staff. It was a policy decision and nothing to do with the work.'

'Nevertheless, two redundancies within three years raises a question mark.'

'If you think it's because I'm no good at the job . . .'

'My dear Richard, I think no such thing. Knowing you as well as I do, I can be quite certain you're highly efficient. What I'm trying to do is to help by seeing things through the eyes of a prospective employer. Then you can approach prepared with answers to all the questions likely to be asked . . . If I've managed to be of some help, I'm very glad.'

'But . . .'

'Yes?'

'I'm asking if you can offer me a job?'

'If *I* can? I'm very sorry, I hadn't realized that's what you wanted.'

Walker-Jones's unctuous manner left Adeane in no doubt that not only had he surmised the purpose of the visit from the beginning – hardly difficult – he enjoyed the evident embarrassment.

'I'm afraid we're too small a firm to employ a full-time PRO; all our publicity is handled by the head salesman. Your talents would just be wasted, which would be a very great shame.'

He could have pleaded, but there was a limit to the humiliation he was prepared to suffer. He stood. 'Thanks, anyway.'

'If I hear of any worthwhile jobs going, Richard, I will, of course, let you know immediately. In the meantime, good luck.'

Adeane left. That 'good luck' had been the final kick to the goolies.

CHAPTER 15

'You really are being a miserable sod.' Patricia used her fork
to spear the last portion of chicken Kiev on her plate. 'For
the past ten minutes, you've done nothing but stare into
space with a constipated look.'

'Give me a little time and I'll find a mental aperient.'

'Bloody funny! What's got you so boring this time?'

'I went along this morning to see my sister-in-law's husband and . . .'

'Why are you always so pompous? He's your brother-in-
law, for God's sake.'

'Strictly speaking, he's not. And I like to keep as great a
distance between us as I can.'

'Why d'you dislike him so much?'

'You wouldn't need to ask if you'd ever met him.'

'Never had the chance, have I? You've never introduced
me.'

'The tangled relationship would cause too many diffi-
culties.'

'You mean they're so grand, you'd be ashamed of me.'

'Rich, but very far from grand. The reason I've never introduced you is simple. Serena and Diana are about as different
as two sisters could be, but they present a united front to
the outside world. Diana could hardly welcome meeting you,
so Serena would go out of her way to be as rude as possible
to you.' Then he added: 'I'd hate to see you embarrassed like
that.'

'I'd give as good as I got . . . If you don't like him, why
d'you go and see him?'

'To ask if he'd give me a job.'

'Did he?'

'No.'

'Why not?'

'He would answer that by saying a successful businessman does not allow personal relationships to cloud his judgements. I would say, for the pleasure of not helping me.'

'Miserable bastard.'

'A description I've no desire to argue with . . . What's the sweet?'

'There may be something in the fridge.'

He went through to the kitchen. There was nothing in the refrigerator and only three tins of rhubarb in the larder. There were many fruits he preferred, but it was her favourite. He opened a tin, emptied the contents into a dish, carried that and a bowl of sugar through to the dining-room. He brought a couple of dessert bowls out of the sideboard.

She helped herself. 'Isn't there any cream?'

'We finished the last yesterday, so unless you bought some today . . .'

Her tone once more became resentful. 'I suppose you think I've had all the time in the world to go shopping?'

'That would depend on whether the intended purchases were considered essential or merely housekeeping.'

'You think that's clever? When you're in this kind of a mood, you're real lousy company.'

'Put it down to my inability to treat the two imposters just the same. I find it so much easier to meet triumph.'

She ate a spoonful of rhubarb. 'Why wouldn't he give you a job? It wouldn't have hurt him to.'

'On the contrary, it would have deprived him of the pleasure of denying me.'

'You always think the worst of people, don't you?'

'It's called, learning from experience.'

'God, you're a laugh a minute!'

They ate.

She broke the silence. 'I'm still hungry. Is there any cheese?'

'There's a piece of mousetrap in the fridge.'

'It's not mousetrap, it's mature cheddar which cost a fortune.'

'Just a description the family used when I was young. Didn't your family have oddball names?'

'No.'

'Chocolate mousse was chocolate sick.'

'That's disgusting.'

'I suppose it is. Can't remember its ever disgusting us so much that we couldn't eat it, though.'

'Aren't you going to get the cheese and biscuits?'

He stood. 'Sorry. I didn't know I was meant to.'

'I have been working all day, you know.'

'Which is why I cheerfully wait on you now.' As he left, he accepted that if he continued to speak to her in the same vein, her antagonism would turn into sulky anger. But if he could not escape the dark shadows that had settled in his mind . . .

He returned to the dining-room, set the cheese and biscuits in front of her, sat.

'Is he really rich?' she asked.

'Tom? So rich he can despise riches.'

'Then he could lend you some money?'

'He could without any bother whatsoever.'

'But you didn't think to ask him to?'

'No.'

'Why not?'

'I had afforded him considerable pleasure by touting for a job; I saw no reason to fill his cup to overflowing.'

'It may make you laugh, talking like that, but if you haven't a job and there's no money, what are you going to do?'

He was tempted to suggest that if she would consider her income as their joint income, they'd slide through; he reached for the cheese instead.

At the press conference in Whitchester, chaired by the deputy chief constable of the county force, each reporter was handed two computer-generated portraits of the murderer and rapist; one in which he wore a wide-brimmed hat and had a bushy moustache, the other without either. As was explained, the first had been composed from witnesses' evidence, the second from the first with the help of experts in facial proportions and bone structures.

A reporter from one of the national newspapers stood. 'So this second likeness is really no more than guesswork based on a portrait that is of a man who, it is admitted, was disguising himself. Isn't that rather ridiculous?'

'I certainly wouldn't put it like that,' replied the deputy chief constable, striving to keep the irritation from his voice. 'One witness was able to give us a very good description. And the experts consulted have had very considerable experience in accurately reconstructing faces.'

A television reporter asked: 'Is the witness you've just referred to one of the earlier victims?'

The deputy chief constable ignored the question. It was possible, he said, that the murderer would try to strike again and therefore every effort had to be made to identify and apprehend him before he did so. As always, the best hope of succeeding lay in securing maximum cooperation from the public. The police were asking anyone, in any part of the country, who had reason to be suspicious of a neighbour, a friend, or even a close relative, to lay aside for once the British dislike of informing and to get in touch with the authorities. Indications that should arouse suspicion were unusual behaviour before and after the dates on which the rapes had taken place, a sudden and inexplicable change of routine, a noticeable alteration in relationships ... People should, while in no sense panicking, take great care not to put themselves at risk; women, especially younger ones, should try not to be on their own after dark in the streets and on no account should they allow themselves to be inveigled into accepting a lift in a car, most especially if the driver had a small dog in it ... The murderer probably was in middle to late middle age; of average to plump build; suffered from a slight speech defect that prevented his pronouncing some words clearly, yet fell short of a lisp; was left-handed; drove old cars, one of which was a Morris Oxford ... A hotline was being set up in Whitchester and calls could be made from any part of the country free of charge; if the caller did not wish to reveal his or her identity, he or she would not be asked to do so.

As Adeane braked to halt in the drive of Turnbull Farm, Amelia ran out of the garden. He climbed out and she hugged him. Before he and Diana had separated, Amelia had never been openly demonstrative; now she was, almost excessively so.

Diana was in the hall and as they said hullo, he felt Amelia's grip on his hand tighten and he sensed she was desperately willing Diana and him to get together again. To her, it must seem so simple a wish to fulfil. Sadly, she would have to grow up before she understood that nothing was so difficult to repair as a relationship between adults. He went forward and kissed Diana on the cheek.

Amelia released his hand. 'Dad, do you want some coffee before we go?'

'He'd love some and so would I,' Diana answered.

'One spoonful of coffee?'

'Two, since we're both having some.'

Amelia hurried into the kitchen. Diana led the way into the sitting-room. 'She made me show her how to make coffee so she could offer you some.'

'Then it's a good job you didn't give me time to say I'd had a cup just before leaving home.'

'Half the art of being a good wife is shutting up her husband in time . . . Bloody hell!'

'A Freudian slip of the tongue.'

'Poor old Freud – gets blamed for everybody's stupidities.' She sat. 'Serena rang on Wednesday, mainly to boast that she was turning in her almost new Volvo for a brand-new Volvo.'

'The advantages of having a husband in the trade.'

'How she'd spit to hear you call it trade! . . . She went on to mention, en passant, that you'd called in to see her.'

'I went there to have a word with Tom.'

'She wouldn't like to hear that either . . . Apparently you wouldn't stay until he arrived home.'

'Safety first.'

'How you men pride yourselves! I've told you, if you were as handsome as Paris, she wouldn't be interested unless you were also as rich as Croesus.'

'Some people are never satisfied.'

'Did you see Tom in the end?'

'At his office on Thursday.'

'Did you ask him for a job?'

'That was the object of the exercise.'

'Some objectives don't get carried out. And you must have found the going very tough.'

'I just about managed to prevent its sticking in my craw.'

'Did he give you a job?'

'No.'

'Oh! I was so hoping . . . He was nice about it, though?'

'He enjoyed every second of my humiliation.'

'Come off it.'

'He played at being dumbly unaware of what I wanted for as long as possible, then, when he finally had to bring the charade to an end, had further fun telling me how sorry he was he couldn't help. I'd no idea he was such a master of hypocrisy.'

'It sounds as if you're letting disappointment and hurt pride talk.'

'However it sounds, that's the way it was.'

'I just don't believe even he could behave so nastily.'

'Your greatest fault has always been that you're too ready to believe the best of people.'

'And yours, that you rush to believe the worst.'

'The only way to survive in the modern-day world.'

'You know that's nonsense. Think badly of someone and the odds are, he'll act badly.'

'Think well and he'll laugh at you.'

'You're not a very nice person when you talk like this.'

Patricia had said much the same thing. Perhaps both of them were right.

'What are you going to do?' she asked after a while.

'Tread the path worn down by all those who've gone before. Try and find an agency who'll handle me because they don't reckon that one automatically becomes senile at forty; look through all the papers and send off to any likely job vacancy; keep my optimism flowing by imagining that out there someone is looking for a PRO just like me.'

'You'll soon find another job.'

'"Who against hope believed in hope."'

'Why not?'

Amelia entered the room, concentrating intently on the tray she carried.

'Put it down here,' Diana said, as she lifted a couple of magazines off an occasional table.

Amelia put the tray down. 'How much sugar, Dad?'

'Three lumps, please. But you know, you should serve ladies first.'

'Mothers are not ladies,' Diana said. 'Go ahead and pour out Daddy's, but give him two lumps, not three, because he needs to lose weight.'

'Who says I do?' he demanded.

'Your trousers are too tight about the waist and . . .' She stopped, furious that once again she had slipped into talking as if in the past.

Amelia put three lumps of sugar into a mug, poured coffee. 'Milk?'

'Please,' Adeane said.

She passed him the mug, stood squarely in front of him. 'Is it nice?'

He drank and wondered if mistakenly she had used something other than coffee. 'It's pure nectar.'

CHAPTER 16

'It's coming up to news time,' Adeane said. 'OK if I change channels?'

'If you must,' Patricia replied.

The newscaster read the headlines. The only time the world was not in a mess, Adeane thought, was when it was in chaos.

World news gave way to domestic news. The Whitchester police were appealing for the public's help in identifying a man they wished to interview in connection with several rapes and the rape and murder of Jane Rowland. Anyone who believed he or she could identify the person in the computer-originated portraits was asked to ring the given free line; callers need not identify themselves if they did not wish to do so. The first picture was on screen for several seconds, then was replaced by the second one.

There seemed to be something familiar about the face, yet irritatingly he couldn't identify what. 'Does this man remind you of anyone?'

Patricia looked up from the magazine through which she had been leafing. 'The bloke on the telly? No. Who is he?'

'The rapist who murdered his last victim.'

'That's great! You reckon I'm friendly with rapists and murderers!'

'I don't think anything of the sort. I just wondered if there was some feature of his face that made you think of someone you know ... it's strange how one can see part of one person's face in someone else's.'

'You may do, I don't.' She returned to the magazine.

The news continued with a brief item about a farmer who had been given a grant to rip up hedges on his thousand acres of farmland, large grants to grow corn, a grant to replace the hedges, a large grant to let the land lie fallow, and now an even larger grant to afforest the land. Adeane decided he should have been a farmer . . .

The phone rang. It was far more likely to be a call for her, but she made no move. He went through to the hall. The call was for her. He returned to the sitting-room. 'Caroline. She says she only wants a very brief word, so see you in half an hour's time.'

Patricia was not amused. She swept out of the room and banged the door shut behind herself. Their relationship was becoming ever more strained, he thought, and accepted that this was largely his fault. She sought the bubbles of life and recently he'd provided none. If he didn't learn to keep the black clouds at bay, he was going to learn the truth of the saying, 'To see the future, look to the past'. Diana and he had broken up largely because he'd been unable to overcome the pressures redundancy had placed on him.

She returned. 'That was Caroline.'

He forbore to point out that he'd told her who the caller was.

She sat. 'You know the trip to France had to be called off because Fred had such a terrible cold?'

'I didn't, no.'

'I told you.'

'Put my loss of memory down to vanishing brain cells.'

'They've decided to make up for it by having a weekend in the Lake District. Don't you think that will be great?'

'Provided they're lucky enough to pick the one weekend in the year when it doesn't rain from Friday through to Monday.'

'They know you're out of work so Caroline –'

'How do they know?'

'I told her. I suppose now you're going to curse me for telling her?'

A man preferred to keep his humiliation private, but he'd promised himself to be pleasant and amusing. 'Of course I'm not. I just wondered, that's all.'

'She's suggested we go with them. And before you start

moaning about the cost, we'll travel in their car and the hotels won't cost a penny.'

'Since when have hoteliers become that altruistic?'

'Fred will take care of the bills. He fiddles them against tax. It's to cheer you up. Don't you think that's wonderfully kind?'

'Very generous.'

'I'll ring back tomorrow and say –'

'Say I'm deeply touched, thanks, but no thanks.'

Her mouth tightened. 'Are you being bloody stupid again?'

'I hope not.'

'They want to be kind, so how do you react? You tell them to shove it.'

'It's easier to give than to receive.'

'That's balls!'

'But true.'

'I'm not surprised that your wife had had enough of you.'

'Nor am I when I stop to think about it.'

'I'm going to bed.' She stood and the magazine dropped from her lap on to the floor. She left, banging the door with even more force than previously.

Peacekeeping had always been a thankless task.

He was not surprised to be met by silence when he entered the bedroom half an hour later. But he was very surprised when, as he climbed into bed, she put her book down, turned to face him, blue eyes wide, lips moist and slightly parted, and said: 'I was beastly, wasn't I?'

'I wouldn't have said that.'

'It's only because I worry so much about you. I do so hate seeing you all despondent. Will you forgive me?' She moved across the bed to snuggle up against him. 'Having you makes me the luckiest woman alive.'

'Only modesty would make me disagree.'

'You must agree with everything I say.'

'I hear and obey.'

'Do you promise to obey me, whatever I want?'

'With the usual proviso that your demands aren't fattening or illegal. There's no objection to immorality.'

'Suppose I tell you to do something very immoral?'

'I've always held that an intelligent man should welcome every new experience.'

The basic experience was not new, but she did introduce a variation that for him was.

She snuggled up against him once more. 'What was it like?'

'Cloud nine was out of sight.'

'Then you feel more cheerful?'

'Life has become golden.'

'It's wonderful when you're like this.' She reached up and kissed him, then slid back to rest her breasts on his chest. She 'nibbled' at his chin with her lips. 'Darling, will you do something for me?'

'If called upon, I'll launch two thousand, not a measly one thousand, ships.'

'Change your mind about going to the Lakes. Think how wonderful it would be.'

He wondered what Helen had really wanted when she'd encouraged Paris?

More and more frequently, he was finding it difficult to fall asleep, even when tired. He turned over and checked the time by the luminous hands of the bedside clock. Twenty to one. He closed his eyes and mentally composed gentle, pastoral scenes, found himself wondering if Patricia really thought him incapable of realizing what had prompted her exotic lovemaking? It was, of course, a thoroughly naive question. She wouldn't care what he realized just so long as he did what she wanted. Then surely it would be equitable to retaliate by expressing further doubts and hesitations, thereby provoking her once more to seduce his agreement? A pattern capable of constant repetition. Had he discovered the route to Shangri-La? . . .

His mind drifted, but irritatingly he still failed to fall asleep. There seemed to be some problem which would not come forward to be identified. Did it concern Amelia? He pictured her the last time he had taken her to the beach. They'd searched for flat pebbles and skimmed these across the calm sea; to her annoyance, she'd never managed more than one touchdown before the pebble had sunk. She'd found a brittle, black egg sac and asked him what this was from and had been surprised when he'd been unable to tell her. She was still young enough to believe him to be omniscient. After leaving the beach, they'd stopped at the ice-cream shop. The rule was, only one ice-cream per outing. She'd had little trouble in wheedling him into buying her a second one. He smiled at the memory of her saying, very seriously, that she wouldn't share the secret even with Taggy, her doll . . . No, there was no problem that concerned her. Diana? It was difficult to think that she could be faced by anything she couldn't quickly sort out on her own. She possessed the self-confidence of someone completely at ease with herself; not religious in the accepted sense, she observed those commandments that ensured she led a good life . . . Serena? When he'd met the sisters for the first time, he'd not looked twice at her. Diana had told him later that this had so surprised her sister – younger, beautiful, she was used to all the attention – that she'd been both annoyed and intrigued. Perhaps Serena's arch manner, suggesting possibilities to an eager mind, was intended to entrap him into making a pass, whereupon she'd slap him down, thereby gaining revenge for his past indifference. Did Serena ever regret having married Tom? Had the price she'd had to pay proved to be too great for the value of what she'd bought? . . .

He finally fell asleep.

The post was delivered ten minutes after Patricia had left for work. He heard the rattle of the flap of the letter box and immediately wondered if he'd find a reply from one of the firms to which he'd sent his CV, offering an interview? . . . Hope was the opium of the fools. It was only nine days since he'd been made redundant, seven since he'd sent off his first application. No firm could be so desperate for his services that they would have replied already.

He went through to the hall. Three letters, all for Patricia. He recognized the handwriting on one of them as being that of a friend of hers who'd stayed with them for several days and almost provoked him into moving to a hotel. Back in the kitchen, he propped the letters up against the toaster, cleared the table, and washed up. He looked through the window to make certain the day remained fine, left home after locking up and walked the mile to the library in the centre of Amersford, gaining some slight degree of self-congratulation from the knowledge that by walking instead of driving, he was saving the cost of petrol, not adding to atmospheric pollution, and taking exercise which was said to be good for modern man.

The public library, a modern, uninspired, two-storey building, lay one road back from Bank Street, on a corner site opposite a memorial garden. On the south side of the ground floor there was a reference section, glassed off from the main area. He entered, nodded at the woman at the desk just inside the door who, despite the fact that he had become a frequent visitor, looked at him with apparent suspicion as if worried he might steal one, or more, of the books under her guardianship. He collected up a copy of each of the newspapers and sat at the long table. He switched on one of the individual lights and began to read through the Jobs Vacant columns.

Hope sprang eternal in the human breast – if it hadn't, there would have been a multitude of suicides. In *The Times* there was an advertisement for a PRO with experience in the motor trade, some French an advantage. His French was almost fluent. A job tailored for him. A sign from above. He wrote down the name and address to which application was to be made. During the next twenty minutes, he noted four more prospects which could be termed promising by an optimist.

He returned his notebook to his pocket and began to read the news. On page three of *The Times* were the two computer portraits of the man the police wished to interview and which had appeared on the television on the previous Saturday night. Below them was a report and a germane article. He read the article, a typical mixture of fact and journalism. Although rape was now considered one of the most heinous of crimes against the person, this had not always been so. In the long past, rulers had seized the favours of any women who took their fancy, irrespective of the ladies' wishes. *Jus prima noctis* had been enthusiastically pursued – against, it had to be assumed, the new bride's wishes – until the time when money had, no doubt with reluctance, been accepted in lieu. In Victorian times, sexual intercourse with a young virgin had been believed to be a cure for venereal disease and many innocents had been sold to be debauched. In surprisingly modern times, women had gone to their wedding bed so ignorant about sex that they had endured what might well be described as rape. The causes of rape were several. The man might suffer some physical defect that made it virtually impossible for him to meet a woman who would willingly have congress with him; he might suffer from a mental aberration . . .

He stopped reading, but continued to stare with unfocused gaze at the newsprint. How could a normal mind comprehend one so abnormal that instead of finding pleasure in willing cooperation, it found it in either actual or simulated resistance? Yet that either there were many such minds or it was a subject with a very wide appeal was surely evidenced by the several films that had been made – always, of course, in the best possible taste – in which one of the participants was shown handcuffed to the bed . . . Even Serena had asked Diana about the practice. Since she was such a prude, it seemed more than a tad strange that she had watched the scene in the film (perhaps she'd put her hands over her eyes, then peeked?), much stranger that she had put the question – hadn't it occurred to her that doing so might well raise in the mind of her listener the thought that her curiosity arose from personal experience? Yet it did call for a quantum leap of imagination to picture Tom, publicly the epitome of arrogant wealth and therefore power, secretly and pathetically needing to pretend to impose his will on an unwilling partner in order to gain his kicks . . .

He abruptly realized why, on Saturday night, when he'd been watching the television and the portraits of the rapist had been shown, some feature had seemed familiar. Now, looking at the photos in front of him, the shape and line of the jaw resembled those of Tom's chin. Tom, the rapist and murderer? Tom was so pompously self-satisfied that it probably would never occur to him that there could be a need to tie down a woman since none would refuse his attentions if he deigned to grant them. Nevertheless, it was an amusing idea, even if less likely than the local vicar's organizing a Walpurgis Night; he laughed to himself as he pictured Tom tying Serena down to the bed . . . He studied the two portraits more closely and decided that the line of the jaw really was similar. But then, as he continued to study them, any similarity seemed to lessen until he was almost convinced there was none. Which made sense since Tom the rapist and murderer was so impossible a projection. Yet it was strange that he was middle aged, slightly overweight, suffered from a very slight speech impediment, and was left-handed . . . Stupid thoughts multiplied like fruit flies. There must be hundreds of thousands of men who were middle aged and overweight; tens of thousands who were left-handed; thousands who had some sort of trouble speaking . . . Yet how many were all of those? And come to remember it, didn't Melly dislike him for no reason she could name other than that he made her feel funny inside? (He could remember saying to Diana that children sometimes could intuitively and without even realizing it, discern the true character of an adult.) And hadn't he been convinced that Tom had delighted in humiliating him when he'd asked for a job . . .

His mind told him he was being ridiculous even as it sought some way of determining the possibility that he was not . . . Serena had said he'd been at Whitchester for a few days. Was that anywhere near Banners Cross, where the murdered girl had lived?

He pushed the chair back, stood, went over to the shelves on which were maps, directories, and atlases. He found a copy of the current AA guide, returned with it to his seat. Whitchester was seventeen miles from Banners Cross. No distance when one was driving. Yet the police said that the murderer of Jane Rowland might have been driving a Morris Oxford, which was about as far downmarket as a Rolls was upmarket, so this thankfully brought an end to all coinci-

101

dences . . . But not to his thoughts. Tom was very successful, very wealthy. Very successful, very wealthy men did not commit crimes. But having told himself that, he went on to call it a knee-jerk reaction. After all, much wealth was garnered through crime, either legal or moral. And great wealth bred delusions of God-like power, of being above the constraints which regulated the lives of all the little people . . .

The police were talking about a serial rapist and had given the dates of the rapes concerned. Then if there were some way of making certain Tom could not have been in the area of one of those rapes, this must finally put a stop to all the absurd, ridiculous, pernicious thoughts which would not leave his head.

CHAPTER 17

Adeane stood in the hall, staring at the phone, calling himself every manner of fool. He was an egregious fool ever to have given the idea credence; a twisted fool to let credence develop into possibility; a weak fool to hesitate at the last moment because it seemed so caddish surreptitiously to check . . .

He lifted the receiver and dialled. He hoped everyone was out; the coward's way was usually the easiest. Pablo answered and said, his diction more mangled than usual, that Señora Alky-Hons was at home and would the señor be kind enough to wait.

'Richard, how nice to hear from you.'

'How nice to hear you say that.'

'I'll bet that look's on your face.'

'What look?'

'When you say something you don't really mean.'

'I'm checking in the mirror and I look indisputably veracious. Scout's honour.'

'Were you ever a scout?'

'In the spirit.'

'If I were in reach, I'd wipe that smile off your face.'

'May I ask how?'

'There's no harm in asking. There might be a lot in answering.'

'Then 'twere best left unsaid for fear of being too much or too little . . . You know I saw Tom last Thursday?'

'Of course. And when he came home, he said how terribly sorry he was. You do understand, don't you?'

'Of course. And I sympathize with the distress it must have caused him . . . The reason for my ringing now is not to moan but to say that he repeated your invitation to a meal.'

'And you're accepting?'

'With pleasure and anticipation.'

'When?'

'I'm not dead certain at the moment and just wanted to make sure you could put up with me. If I may, I'll get in touch again to fix a day just as soon as I know what's what.'

'Don't you always know?'

'Not when life becomes complicated.'

'It's the complications that make it interesting, surely?'

'As long as they don't become dangerous . . . By the way, just before I ring off, you can earn me a fiver.'

'Shouldn't it be the other way around?'

'I've had a bet with a friend who swears he saw Tom in Swansea on the twenty-second of last month.'

'Impossible. He's never been near the place.'

'Can you be absolutely certain he wasn't there?'

'I can check in his appointments diary. Hang on whilst I go through to the library.'

He waited. There was a click as a second receiver was lifted.

'From the twentieth to the twenty-fourth, he was in Manchester on business.'

'Then the fiver's mine.'

'Why were you so certain it wasn't him that you bet on it?'

'Now, I can reveal all! The man my friend saw was in a night club with two bimbos who were young enough to be his daughters. Since anyone married to you wouldn't be attracted by a dozen bimbos, I knew my friend had to be wrong.'

'You're sweet!'

'Sometimes, that's easy.'

'How are you going to spend your winnings?'

'I thought maybe I'd buy someone a box of chocolates.'

'Am I allowed to ask who that someone is?'

'You are not. But you do like truffles, don't you?'

She laughed. 'You will be along soon, won't you? And you'll be on your own?'

The less-than-subtle way of telling him Patricia would not be welcome. 'I will.'

He said goodbye, replaced the receiver. On the twenty-second of June, Tom had been staying within easy driving distance of Bledstone, where the previous rape victim had lived.

How many coincidences did there have to be before they ceased to be coincidences? Surely life proved that, especially when seen in retrospect, there could be any number? Then did he accept that this was so and remain silent, thereby avoiding any unpleasantness to anyone? This must be by far the most welcome choice. Yet, his conscience insisted on asking, was he prepared to take it when he must know that there might be one or more women who in the future would become victims if he failed to tell the police what he had learned . . . ?

He returned to the hall, lifted the receiver, dialled the number he had noted.

A woman said: 'You are speaking to the special unit set up by the county constabulary to receive information concerning the rape and murder of Jane Rowland and the rapes of three other women which occurred on the sixteenth of September, last year, near Treighley; the twenty-third of May this year, near Greencastle; and the twenty-second of June, near Bledstone. If you do not wish to give your name and address, you do not have to. Please now go ahead and provide any information you may have.'

Conscious that his voice was strained, he said: 'I know a man who is middle aged, slightly overweight, left-handed, and has a slight speech impediment. He was in Whitchester at the time of the murder and was staying in Manchester in June when that rape took place. It is possible he ties his wife down to the bed before having sexual intercourse.'

'Will you please identify this person and give me any more details you can.'

Detective Inspector Barnard reached across the desk and lifted the receiver. 'Detective Inspector.'

'Dawes. I've just received a call from the Oaksprite rape unit. They've had an anonymous tip-off naming Thomas Walker-Jones of Farthingstone House, Upper Lington, as a possible suspect. Do you know anything about the man?'

'No, sir, but I'll find out what I can.'

'Get back on to me as soon as possible.'

Barnard replaced the receiver, rubbed his square chin. The name had rung a bell, but he hadn't been able immediately to identify why. He still couldn't.

He left his room and went into the next one. 'If I say Thomas Walker-Jones of Farthingstone House, what do you say?'

'Mine's a sky-blue Azure.' Detective Sergeant Eason, who'd been laboriously typing with three fingers, sat back in his chair.

The D I settled on the corner of the desk. 'Would you care to explain?'

'Royal Motors is owned by Walker-Jones and they'll sell you a Bentley Azure if you've got a couple of hundred thousand in the bank.'

'Of course! Well, he's hardly likely to be our target . . . The D C S has had word from Oaksprite that there's been an anonymous tip-off naming him.'

'It'll have been some dissatisfied customer whose Rolls broke down.'

'That's close to treason. Rollers don't break down.'

The relationship between the two men was an easy one, perhaps because they were so opposite in character. The D I was young for his rank, full of ambition, but short of hard experience because he had joined the force on the fast track as a graduate; the detective sergeant was old for his rank, had lost all ambition, and had a fund of hard experience. It was to the D I's credit that from the beginning he had been prepared to evaluate any advice or opinion Eason gave that ran counter to his own thinking, never seeing this as in any sense diminishing his authority.

Barnard slid off the desk. 'Find out if any of the lads know Upper Lington and can fill us in in any way.' He left.

Twenty minutes later, there was a quick knock on his door and Eason stepped into the room, followed by a man in uniform. 'P C Snow, guv'nor. Lives in Tycefield, the next village to Upper Lington; says he knows Farthingstone House.'

Barnard looked up at the young, square-faced PC who had a full beard, well trimmed. 'What can you tell me about the place and the man?'

'It's a real mansion, sir; must cost a bomb to run. Mr Walker-Jones is very wealthy. Not popular in the village because he tries to lord it and even though he coughs up for local people, he never gives as much as someone in his position should. Married to a lovely bit of crackling, half his age.'

'Presumably she keeps him occupied . . . Right, thanks.'

The PC turned smartly, left.

'A bummer of a tip-off,' Barnard said.

Before he could phone the detective chief superintendent to report, a fax from county HQ was brought to him. He read it through. He was glad he had not had time to make that phone call because the transcript of the anonymous tip-off made it clear that it was not, perhaps, quite such a bummer after all. Walker-Jones would have to be interviewed. But since wealthy men disliked being asked questions by the police, it surely would be to the point to persuade the detective chief superintendent that in view of the social and financial standing of the person concerned, he should be in charge of the interview. Then if shit did hit the fan, he'd be the one to be splattered.

CHAPTER 18

Detective Chief Superintendent Dawes's normal expression had been likened to that of a St Bernard which had accidentally dropped its barrel of brandy down a crevasse. He looked round the green sitting-room into which they'd been shown by Pablo. 'Quite some place!'

'It's that,' agreed Barnard, not expressing his own opinion that the room had the stilted touch of a provincial museum about it, not least because of the pair of bow-fronted display cabinets which were crammed with figurines that no doubt were worth a fortune, but said nothing to him.

Dawes crossed to the nearest eight-foot window and stared out. 'Some garden!'

The DCS, Barnard thought, seemed slightly ill at ease in surroundings of such wealth. Or maybe he was just worried about what course the forthcoming interview would take.

One of the three doors opened and Walker-Jones entered. He crossed the carpet to stand in front of the large fireplace with its elaborately carved marble surround.

Barnard, who was the first to admit that instant character assessment was more likely to be wrong than right, placed him as cocky, aggressive, and ready to bully anyone who'd allow himself to be bullied.

Dawes spoke with considerable respect. 'Kind of you to see us, Mr Walker-Jones. Sorry we've had to bother you.'

'Why have you?'

'We're making certain inquiries and believe you may be able to help us with them.'

'Most unlikely. We only handle previously owned cars when there can be no doubt whatsoever about their provenance.'

Barnard was amused by this suggestion that luxury cars were more art than commerce.

'Our inquiries do not concern cars,' Dawes said.

'Then I fail to understand why you're bothering me.'

He suffered from only a very slight speech defect, Barnard noted; sometimes it was just evident, more often it was not. It seemed logical to suppose that when under intense emotional strain, it would be more in evidence.

'Our inquiries concern the rape of three women and the rape and murder of Miss Jane Rowland.'

Walker-Jones's expression blanked.

'You have read or heard about these incidents, I imagine?'

'Are you trying to suggest I have any knowledge concerning them?'

'That is what I hope to find out.'

'You are being impertinent.'

'Not intentionally, sir, I can assure you.'

'It is the greatest possible impertinence to suggest I could know anything at all about them.'

'Countrywide inquiries are being carried out and a great number of people are being interviewed, not because they are in any way suspected, but because they might be able to provide either positive or negative evidence that will prevent us pursuing a useless line of inquiry. Can you understand that?'

'Of course I understand what you're saying. But what I fail utterly to understand is why you think I can offer any evidence, positive or negative.'

'I hope that that will soon become clear. Have you ever met any of the victims?'

'No.'

'On the first of this month, were you driving towards the hamlet of Mainton and just before you reached there did you stop to offer a woman a lift?'

'No.'

'Where were you on the first of this month between ten-forty-five and eleven at night?'

'Here, at home. Superintendent, I am a very busy man so whilst I naturally would wish to be able to help, since I cannot, this meeting must end.' He turned, reached across and pressed a bell at the side of the fireplace.

Confirmation he was left-handed, Barnard noticed.

'I'm sorry, sir,' Dawes said, 'but I do have one or two more questions to ask you.'

Walker-Jones turned back. 'They must go unanswered.'

'I insist . . .'

'In my house, I do the insisting. Anything more can be said to my solicitors who will doubtless point out that there is only a thin line between making pointed inquiries and slanderous inferences.'

A door opened and Pablo entered.

'Perhaps you'll at least tell us if you have any dogs in the house?'

'We have none because my wife does not like them . . . Show them out,' he said to Pablo.

'Thank you for your help, sir,' Barnard said, with polite sarcasm.

As they drove between the oaks towards the road, Dawes said: 'Well?'

'There is a slight resemblance between him and the computer portraits.'

'Bloody slight.'

'He's middle aged, left-handed, and suffers from a slight speech defect.'

'So?'

'He didn't like the questions and I'd say that wasn't solely a case of puffed-up pride.'

They reached the gateway and Dawes braked to a halt, checked the road was clear, drew out. 'When you see a place like that, it's easy enough to imagine the owner as a swindler. It's difficult to see him as a rapist and murderer.'

'Just because a man's stinking rich, it doesn't mean his mind can't be as twisted as a corkscrew.'

'I know that,' Dawes said, irritated. 'But whatever a rich man wants, he'll find someone who'll give it to him at a price. Why would he risk raping when he can buy?'

'Because if you buy, there's no real resistance, only simulated. Genuine resistance and the fear that goes with it offer a unique pleasure.'

'How the hell d'you know that?'

'I had a word with a psychiatrist.'

'So how the hell does he know? . . . If you were asked for a flash verdict on him, based on nothing more concrete than we've got, what would it be?'

'He's a distinct possible.'

'Instinct can be hellish wrong . . . What evidence there is says the rapist drives around in an old car. Would a bloke like him even know there was once a car called the Morris Oxford?'

'He is in the car business.'

'That's like saying Dior is in the rag trade.'

'The virtual lack of any incriminating evidence shows the rapist/murderer is smart. A smart man would know that despite every precaution, the car might be identified so he decides that each time he uses a different one and afterwards it's junked. Walker-Jones would have very little difficulty in setting things up.'

They slowed, turned right on to the main road to Amersford.

'He's going to have to be pressured into answering more questions,' Dawes said slowly. 'Can you recall the info that came through from Oaksprite?'

'Not word for word, but in broad terms, yes.'

'The informant claims Walker-Jones was in Manchester from the twentieth to the twenty-fourth of June and in Whitchester on the first of this month. Is that how you remember things?'

'Yes.'

'Assume Walker-Jones is the rapist. He's very smart and he's worked out how to commit rape, and murder, without leaving any traces that could incriminate him. But people who know they're very smart often reckon everyone else is dumb and unable to think laterally. Show that he was in the vicinity of the other two rapes and he'd be under pressure. If we ask him where he was at the relevant times, we'll get nowhere. But he may well have gone ahead and, as usual, stayed at the most luxurious hotel in the area on each occasion ... Start finding out if he did.'

Understanding that the appearance of being a philanthropist was more important than actually being one, Walker-Jones had always made certain that his donations to charity were to high-profile organizations since then his generosity was likely to be well recorded. This had ensured that his photograph frequently appeared in socially orientated magazines.

DC Bissell, seated on his desk in the CID general room, began to search through half a dozen magazines. Within a couple of minutes, he said aloud: 'What an ugly bastard!'

DC Fishburn, at the next desk, looked across. 'If the view's that worrying, turn the mirror over.'

'Remind me to laugh when I've the time.' He read the caption below the half-page colour photograph. 'What does one do with his sort of money?'

'If you don't know, pass it on to someone who does ... What's got you all excited?'

'The guv'nor wants a photo of Walker-Jones and it says here that he's a multi-millionaire.'

'What's the interest?'

'Didn't say, but since he's been with the DCS for part of the morning and has come back shouting, it's big – like as not, the Steps Wood murder.'

Not long afterwards, a WPC, who had considerable artistic talent, was called into the DI's office and asked to paint a reproduction of the photograph and then to add a moustache and wide-brimmed hat.

The younger receptionist at the Queen's Hotel in Edinburgh said: 'Hang on a sec, will you?'

As he waited, the DC studied the people who passed through the foyer. It astounded him that there were so many who could afford a hundred pounds a night for a bed and fifty pounds a head for dinner. Come the revolution, they'd all be dossing down in shop doorways and it would be he who'd be living it up in the hotel.

A small, elderly man, wearing a black coat and striped

trousers, hair receding in a crescent so that at first glance it looked as if he were wearing a cap tipped to the back of his head, passed through a doorway and up to the counter. 'You'd better come through, Constable.' He lifted the counter flap.

There were two desks in the office and at one of these a woman worked. The DC was given a chair to sit on.

Once seated behind the second desk, the assistant manager said: 'I hope this doesn't mean any sort of trouble?'

'Just a routine inquiry. Can you say whether a Mr Thomas Walker-Jones was staying here on the sixteenth of September last year?'

'Your reason for asking?'

'My boss is a morose sort of bloke and didn't tell me.'

'I hope he, and you, understand that we do like to respect the confidences of our guests?'

'Sure. So tell me in confidence.'

The assistant manager hesitated, then turned to the secretary. 'Would you please see if we still have the guest list for the sixteenth of September of last year, Miss Yates?'

She tapped out instructions on a keyboard, read the VDU. 'Yes, we have.'

'Was a Mr Thomas Walker-Jones staying here?'

She input more instructions, the display changed. 'He was booked in from the fourteenth to the seventeenth.'

The salesman in Royal Motors looked pained. 'We have never handled a Morris Oxford of any age.'

'Surely,' the DC said, 'when a bloke buys a new car, he slings in his old one in part exchange?'

'We naturally like to do our best to assist a client in the purchase of a new car. However, even if a client did possess such a car as you have described, I am quite certain he would not ask us to dispose of it.'

As the CID Escort came to a stop, Eason looked through the driving window. 'I used to daydream about owning a cottage like this.'

Barnard said: 'What brought the dream to a stop?'

'I grew up.'

'You can be a miserable sod!'

'It's that what keeps me cheerful. That and the thought that old houses suffer from woodworm, deathwatch beetle, wet and dry rot, and the water pipes are made from lead and are poisoning the inhabitants.'

'Let's move before you have me cutting my throat to cheer myself up.'

They left the car and walked up the brick path, past colourful flowerbeds and a small lawn that was first cousin to a bowling green, to the front door. Eason rang the bell.

Pamela Turner opened the door to the extent of a chain. 'Yes?'

'Detective Inspector Barnard and Detective Sergeant Eason, county constabulary, Mrs Turner. Here's my warrant card.' Eason held it so that she could see it through the gap.

The door was shut to enable the chain to be disengaged, then opened fully. 'Sorry for the delay, but these days one has to be so careful,' she said.

'It's nice to see that you are.'

'Come on in.'

They entered.

'How can I help you?' she asked.

'We'd like you to look at a sketch.'

'Let's go into the sitting-room. And would you like some coffee?'

'Thanks, but we won't.'

They went into the small sitting-room. Once seated, she said: 'Is this sketch of the man who stopped and offered me a lift?'

'That's what we're hoping you'll tell us,' Barnard answered.

'Was he the rapist?'

'We don't yet know.'

'I still . . . I know it's silly, but I still shiver inside when I think about it.'

'Nothing silly about that, I can assure you.'

'But if he was the rapist and murderer, I'm frightening

myself over what might have happened, but didn't; if he wasn't, I'm making a fool of myself.'

'Will it help if I tell you that in similar circumstances most people worry to a far greater degree than I imagine you do?'

'A doubtful consolation! If you've broken your leg, you're lucky; you might have broken your neck.'

'When you can joke about things, Mrs Turner, you're doing all right.' He turned to Eason. 'Let's have the sketch.'

Eason opened the large brown envelope he'd been carrying and brought out the photograph of the sketch the WPC had made. He handed it to her.

'Take all the time you want,' Barnard said.

She studied the photograph. 'I imagine you want a definite yes or no?'

'If that's possible?'

'I don't think it is. On a scale of one to ten, it's nine he is the man who was in the car. But it was dark, I was cursing my car, and then I started becoming scared. I just can't remember as clearly as I want.'

'Not to worry,' Barnard said. Nine out of ten wasn't good enough for the witness-box, but it convinced him that when her judgement was added to the other evidence, Walker-Jones was their target.

CHAPTER 19

Adeane rang the bell. After only a couple of seconds, Amelia opened the door and hugged him. 'How are things?' he asked.

'Rowena had a party yesterday and ate so many coconut kisses she was sick.'

'An early introduction into the perils of enjoyment.'

She released him. 'I don't know what that means. Why do you sometimes talk funnily?'

'It runs in the genes; your grandfather used to annoy your grandmother because he would keep punning. Do you know what a pun is?'

'Talking funnily?'

'One always hopes so. Are you ready for the off, all pennies spent so that we don't have to stop in the most impossible place?'

'Of course,' she said scathingly. 'But don't you want some coffee first?'

He remembered the taste of the coffee she had previously served. 'I don't think there's really time . . .'

She took hold of his hand. 'Mummy said you'd want some.' She pulled.

As he followed her into the hall, he wondered whether she was old enough to reason that if he and Diana saw more of each other they might come together, still young enough to believe that possible? He could see Diana in the kitchen. ''Morning. Melly says there's coffee on the menu?'

'I thought you might like some before leaving.'

She had spoken casually but, thanks to the telepathy there sometimes seemed to be between them, he was certain she wanted to tell him something. 'I would indeed.'

'Any news of a job?'

'Not yet, but hope eternal continues to spring.'

'Melly wrote a letter to Santa Claus asking him to find you a job, but she's worried that she can't post it until the end of the year.'

He said to Amelia: 'That kind of letter can be posted any day.'

'Then I'm going to give it to Mummy so she can post it tomorrow.'

'Tell her to send it express.'

'What does that mean?'

'Two more reindeer than usual to make certain it goes faster.'

Diana called out: 'Why don't you go into the sitting-room? I'll bring the coffee through when it's made.'

'I'll make it,' Amelia said.

'Daddy wants to see your scrapbook, so you show him that while I fix things.'

He followed Amelia into the sitting-room where she proudly showed him the scrapbook she had just started. A few minutes later, Diana entered. He took the tray from her and put it down on the occasional table. She poured the coffee, added milk and sugar to one mug, milk only to another, handed him the first. As she sat, she said: 'Melly, it's such a lovely day, why not go out and enjoy the sun until it's time to go?'

'I don't want to get melon.'

'Melon? . . . Oh! Melanoma. You only get that if you spend hours and hours in the very hot sun. A little sunshine now can only do you good, especially if you wear the hat I bought you the other day.'

'I don't think I like it.'

'I suppose it does make you look rather grown up.'

'Does it?'

'I think so.'

'Oh! Maybe I will wear it.'

'You might see Mr Frog down by the sandpit.'

'Really?'

117

'Didn't I tell you I saw him earlier on, hoppitying all over the place?'

Amelia hurried out of the room.

As they heard the front door shut, Diana said: 'And the next time I catch Melly fibbing, I'll tick her off! Who was it said that the best parent is the smartest hypocrite? . . . You're never going to guess what's happened.'

'Then I won't even try.'

'Spoilsport! Serena rang up the other day in a terrible state to say the police had been questioning Tom. And you know why?'

'I suppose his firm has inadvertently handled a stolen Rolls or Ferrari.'

'Because they seem to think he may know something about the awful rapes and murder.'

'Then they have to be out of their tiny little minds.'

She drank. 'Are you all that surprised?' she asked, as she put the mug down.

'What's that supposed to mean?'

'You just don't seem as surprised as I'd have expected.'

That damned mental telephone! 'If I could believe it to be even remotely possible, I'd be totally gobsmacked. As it is, I'm rather amused.'

'Serena doesn't find it funny.'

'Amusing incredible, not amusing funny. Anyway, I'm sure that, as usual, she'll have got all her facts wrong.'

'How could she with something like that?'

'I don't know. But if there's a way, she'll have found it.'

'Stop being smart. She says they've also been asking questions at the two showrooms. They wanted to know if a Morris Oxford had ever been taken in part exchange.'

'Where's the relevance of that?'

'Don't you remember that when the police were asking for information, they said the rapist may have been driving a Morris Oxford?'

'I had forgotten.'

Amelia returned. 'Mr Frog wasn't there.'

'I expect he'll be back later on,' Diana said.

'Then shall I put out some bread and milk for him?'

She turned to Adeane. 'Do frogs eat bread and milk?'

'I haven't the faintest idea. Let's see if we can find out from the encyclopaedia when I've finished my coffee.'

In the interview room, Barnard, seated at the side of the detective chief superintendent, listened to Belling's mellifluous voice and thought that all might be equal in the eyes of the law, but when you could afford a top lawyer, you were a bloody sight more equal.

'So you will understand, Superintendent, that while my client would normally and naturally have resented his having been asked to come here, because he appreciates the circumstances are far from normal, he sees it to be his duty to comply with your request in the hopes that, however unlikely, he may be of some assistance.' Belling was the quintessential English gentleman; Turnbull and Asser shirt, Anderson and Sheppard suit, Echona shoes, and slightly grubby old Etonian tie. 'My understanding is that you have certain questions you wish to put to him?'

'That's so.'

'What is their rationale?'

'I think Mr Walker-Jones may be able to help us in our investigations.'

'What leads you to that conclusion?'

'Certain evidence.'

'Perhaps you will enumerate it.'

'It will become clear from the questions.'

'I think that in fairness to my client, you should put all your cards on the table at the beginning; makes for so much fairer a game.'

The word 'game', Barnard thought sourly, had been deliberately introduced; should the recording being made ever be heard in court, the jury would understand that the defence had never considered it necessary to take the allegations too seriously.

'The special incident room received a call in which Mr Walker-Jones was named as the rapist and murderer.'

'Did the caller identify himself?'

'No, he didn't.'

'Then my client has been asked to come here in response to an anonymous telephone call; anonymous, because the caller obviously did not wish to be questioned as to his motivation or as to the validity of what he had to say.'

'I can have no knowledge as to his motive.'

'The conclusion is inescapable.'

'I think, sir, at the moment that can be no more than a matter of opinion.' Dawes turned to face Walker-Jones. 'Can you remember where you were on the sixteenth of September of last year?'

'No.' His tone was as curt as his answer.

'Superintendent,' Belling said, with continuing cool, infuriatingly superior politeness, 'could you say where you were on a particular day almost a year ago?'

'If I consulted my work diary, yes.'

'And if my client consulted his last year's appointments diary, it is possible he could answer. In the meantime, he cannot.'

'Then if I say he was staying at the Queen's Hotel, in Edinburgh, he will not deny that?'

'Surely it is clear that he cannot confirm or deny it?'

'Then we'll move on to the twenty-third of May of this year. Mr Walker-Jones, where were you on that day?'

'I do not know.'

'Then you cannot deny that you were staying at the Beacon Hill Hotel in Newcastle?'

'He can neither confirm nor deny it,' said Belling.

'On the twenty-second of June, were you staying at the Rock Hotel in Manchester?'

'I do not know.'

'On the first of July, were you staying at the Royal Clarence Hotel in Whitchester?'

'I do not know.'

'The first of July is only just over a fortnight ago. I would have thought you'd remember whether –'

'My client,' cut in Belling, 'is a very busy man who in the course of his work frequently travels around the country; in such circumstances, it is totally reasonable for him to be uncertain where he was with the exactitude that you are demanding. Why are the questions considered to be in any way relevant?'

'A lady, who lives in Treighley, fifteen miles from Edinburgh, was raped on the sixteenth of September; a lady, who lives in Greencastle, twenty-one miles from Newcastle, was raped on the twenty-third of May; a lady, who lives in Bledstone, was raped on the twenty-second of June and the dog in the car of the rapist was probably stolen from Kington, which is six miles from Manchester; Miss Rowland, who lived in Banners Cross, was raped and murdered on the first of this month in Steps Wood which is seventeen miles from Whitchester.'

'Are you suggesting that these facts hold any particular significance for my client?'

'On each occasion, he was staying at a hotel not far from the scene of the crime.'

'Coincidence.'

'In the force, we have a saying, twice, coincidence, thrice, extraordinary, four times, *Guinness Book of Records*.'

'It is to be hoped that the intelligence with which the investigation is being carried out is greater than that of the author of such nonsense . . . I presume that every male who was staying at the Queen's Hotel on the sixteenth of September has been interviewed; as has every male who was staying on one of the relevant dates at the other hotels?'

'They have not.'

'Then you cannot know how many other men were also staying at all these hotels on the relevant dates.'

'It's very unlikely . . .'

'You cannot *know*, can you?'

'No.'

'Had a thorough investigation ever been contemplated, that fact undoubtedly would have been one of the first to be ascertained. That it has not been must suggest a vendetta is being waged against my client, probably because in this day and age the ethos of equality holds that great success is to be denigrated.'

'It is ridiculous to suggest a vendetta by the police.'

'Far less absurd, I assure you, than suggesting that a man

of my client's proven integrity and position in society, a noted benefactor, very happily married, could be both a rapist and a murderer. There can be no point in continuing this interview.'

'I still have a few questions.'

'Then I suggest you ask them as quickly as possible. And it is to be hoped that they are very much more relevant than those already put to my client.'

Barnard, at a sign from Dawes, said: 'What cars do you and your wife own, Mr Walker-Jones?'

'I have a Rolls Royce and my wife has a Volvo.'

'Do your servants have a car?'

'I bought them a Peugeot last year.'

'Was it new?'

'Of course.'

'Have you owned a Morris Oxford in the past two months?'

'No.'

'Have you driven a Morris Oxford in the past two months?'

'No.'

'Do you own any company or business other than Royal Motors?'

'No.'

'Do you have an interest in any other company or business which is concerned with cars?'

'My client has just answered that question,' Belling said.

'Not exactly. I . . .'

'My client has very willingly given you his full cooperation, wishing, as any right-minded citizen must, to provide all the help he can to those investigating such ghastly crimes. However, he is an exceedingly busy man and since it has become obvious there is nothing he can usefully tell you, this interview can be concluded.' He stood, carefully packed papers into his briefcase. 'Good morning, gentlemen.' He and Walker-Jones left.

Barnard spoke into the tape recorder to close the interview, switched it off. 'That bastard mouthpiece is so smooth, he'd spread straight out of the fridge . . . You didn't challenge Walker-Jones with tying his wife down to the bed before he humps her.'

'I thought about it,' Dawes replied, 'but came to the conclusion there was no point in doing so at this stage. He'd have denied doing any such thing, the mouthpiece would have accused us of merely trying to blacken his character, and he'd have learned we know about his possible funny little ways. Far better for prosecuting counsel to spring the news in court and leave him gasping and his wife in tears. If the jury are typical, they'll condemn him all ends up for indulging in something they've never had the chance to try.'

Patricia had left Adeane to cook the frozen steak-and-kidney pie, peas, and chips in the microwave; she remained seated as he cleared the plates.

'No one's offered you a job,' she said.

As he put the cheese on the table, he thought that in the ranks of the obvious, her remark scored highly.

'When's someone going to?'

'When all the CVs are thrown up into the air and mine is lucky and lands on top of the pile.'

'What if it never does?'

'I never consider the impossible,' he answered. He was not surprised when she missed the irony of his answer.

'We can't go on for ever like this.'

'Fear not. Only diamonds are for ever.'

'How bloody typical! I'm worried sick and all you can do is joke. You know your trouble, don't you? You're . . .' She stopped as the phone began to ring. She pushed the chair back and stood. 'That'll be June; she promised to ring back.' She went through to the hall.

He helped himself to cheese, a biscuit, and butter. He found many of her friends difficult to get on with, but June was different. She was down to earth, cheerfully content, and not very well off. Added to which, she was an enthusiastic cook.

Patricia returned. 'It's for you,' she said bad temperedly, as she sat.

'Who is it?'

'Her.'

He went through to the hall, picked up the receiver. 'Is there trouble?'

'No,' Diana replied. 'Why d'you think there might be?'

'It's quite late in the evening for you to be ringing.'

'Melly and I have been out and it was only after I got back that Serena rang and got through. I thought you'd like to hear the news. Sorry if I alarmed you.'

'Alarm over. So what is the latest scandal?'

'Tom was asked to go along to be questioned at the police station. It seems they really do think he might be the rapist.'

'Why so?'

'Each time a woman's been raped, he was staying in a nearby hotel. They questioned him about cars, wanting to know if he's ever owned or driven a Morris Oxford. And does he own any company other than Royal Motors that deals in cars?'

'What did they say when he told them about the scrap firms?'

'He won't have told them. As I said to you, he's ashamed of owning them, even though they're money spinners. All right, that's really stupid, but most of us are really stupid about something . . . How can the police even begin seriously to suspect him?'

'There was that anonymous phone call you told me about. And there are several coincidences – he's middle aged, a bit overweight, left-handed, has a slight speech defect, and now it appears he was staying somewhere near where each rape and the murder took place.'

'For God's sake, Dick, I know you don't like him, but do you have to let dislike warp your judgement so much?'

'I was merely trying to answer you by putting the facts as the police must see them.'

There was a brief pause. 'I shouldn't have said that; it wasn't fair. Forgive?'

'Forgotten.'

'It's small wonder Serena's half out of her mind, isn't it? I mean, what can they do to stop this absurd persecution?'

'Surely Tom's got hold of a high-powered solicitor?'

'Serena say's he's employing the very best; the chap went with him to the police station.'

'Then there's nothing more he can or need do. But she'll

have to calm down and realize it's not persecution, it's merely the police carrying out their duty.'

'Is it their duty to infer he's a rapist and a murderer? I thought one was innocent until proven guilty?'

'That's in court. The average policeman finds it difficult to believe anyone's innocent. But sooner or later they'll come round to accepting that Tom is.'

'I hope you're right.'

'I usually am.'

'Self-satisfaction is the eighth deadly sin . . . I must go and do the cooking.'

'What's for supper?'

'Farmer's Pride – puff pastry on top of leeks, cheese, and bacon. Do you remember?'

'So vividly that I'm salivating.'

'Compliments should always be restrained. And I'll bet you're going to have something just as nice for your supper.'

He wondered if she believed that or was fishing. *'Escalopes de foie gras frais poèlées.'*

'Lies should be equally restrained unless one's a mother. I must go now or Melly will be asleep before it's time to eat . . . She's shouting to say she sends her love, and kisses from Teddy.'

'Love returned, but I'd rather Teddy had a bath before he becomes that intimate.'

They said goodbye.

When he returned to the dining-room, Patricia said fretfully: 'That was a hell of a long call.'

He sat. By her standard it had been little more than a brief chat.

'I can't think what you find to talk about.'

'Melly, most of the time.'

'You spoil your daughter.'

'Where's the point in being young if you're not spoilt?'

He had expected to find the second anonymous call easier to make because practice was said to grease the path of a guilty conscience. But it didn't work out like that. He stood by the table in the hall and absurdly found himself searching for a reason not to phone. Yet, Goddamnit, by giving the information all he'd be doing was helping the police uncover the truth and that was the duty of any honest citizen . . .

He finally picked up the receiver, dialled. When the woman at the other end of the line had finished speaking, he said: 'Walker-Jones owns a company which is probably registered in or near Gloucester and deals in scrap metal; it has several sites around the country and handles cars.'

When he replaced the receiver, he was sweating.

The scene epitomized the throwaway society; battered, rusting cars were piled one on top of another in huge squares. The police Escort braked to a halt in front of the wooden office.

'What a dump!' said the younger PC, as he released the seat belt.

'Sure. But where there's muck, there's brass,' replied the elder PC.

They stepped out of the car. From somewhere to their right came the screech of tortured metal, from their left, an intermittent hammering. A fork-lift truck, with an unusually high lift, came up the track they'd just used and passed them.

They crossed to the office and climbed the three steps, entered a square office in which worked a young woman whose exaggerated hair and clothes style did not flatter her looks. She said pertly: 'Look who's here!'

'Two handsome coppers,' said the younger PC.

'You mean there's more of you?'

'Is the boss in?' asked the elder PC.

'I'll see.' She stood, crossed to the inside door, went through.

'It's not all junk here, then,' said the younger PC, having watched her leave.

She returned. 'He'll see you.'

They went through into a second office, sparsely furnished. Lynes came round the desk and shook hands with apparent enthusiasm. A small, round, rubbery man, he combined a warm manner, a ready smile, and an air of slight deference, all of which were false. 'So, gentlemen, sit down and tell me what brings you here. Trouble? As I always say, life is spelt with a capital T.' He returned to his chair behind the desk. 'You smoke?' He picked up a wooden box, lifted the lid.

'We don't, thanks all the same,' replied the elder PC.

'Heading for a long life! Wish I was, but can't take the extra stress of giving up fags. If it means I have to go early, that's my karma.' He took a cigarette out of the box, lit it. 'So how can I help?'

'You know Mr Walker-Jones, don't you?'

Shutters seemed to come down behind Lynes's eyes. 'Who's that?'

'The register of companies says he owns Jones and Son of this address.'

'Is that so?'

'When's the last time he was here?'

'I don't recollect saying he ever had been.'

'You wouldn't be trying to dazzle us, would you?'

'God forbid.'

'Then cut out the bullshit. Tell us when he was last here.'

Lynes considered the situation for a while, then said: 'I'd have to check the records.'

'Get checking.'

He swivelled his chair round, pulled open the top drawer of a cabinet and brought out a file. He put this down on the desk, read one of the papers inside. 'May the fourth.'

'Give over. It's July now. Are you trying to make out he doesn't bother to keep an eye on things?'

'If I told you that, I'd be lying. He has accountants what come in and look at the books so often it seems like they're part of the business. But he don't come here in person very often. Straight, May's the last time.'

'Has he ever driven off in one of the cars waiting to be junked?'

'Am I hearing straight? You can think a bloke who owns a hundred thousand quids' worth of Rolls is going to come here for a car that's for scrapping and worth zilch?'

'At the beginning of this month, did he bring in a Morris Oxford for scrapping?'

'I'm not making sense.' He stubbed out the cigarette.

'You'll see angels shopping in Marks and Sparks for haloes before he does that.'

'You get cars left outside the gates, don't you?'

'That's right. By blokes what haven't the energy to come in and ask us to handle 'em.'

'Did you find an Oxford outside the gates at the beginning of this month?'

'How can I remember every car?'

'By trying.'

'Gentlemen, I'd like to help. As I always say, law and order is all that separates us from the savages. But to save me becoming a savage, I couldn't give you an answer. I just can't remember. It's as simple as that. You wouldn't want me to lie, would you, instead of being honest?'

'How would we tell the difference?'

'Come on, don't be like that.'

'Maybe one of the blokes who works for you will have a better memory.'

'Ask 'em. But the only thing any of 'em ever remembers is what day is pay day.'

Pinning down a blob of quicksilver would be easier, the elder PC thought.

The detective chief superintendent's office was on the fourth floor of county HQ. The personal items in it provided an insight into his off-duty character which was both predictable and unpredictable. On the desk was a leather holder containing three photographs of his family; on the mantelpiece of the blocked-up fireplace was a model oar, mounted on a low plinth, which recorded that Anthony Dawes had been a member of the crew which had won the southern counties eights many years previously; in the bookcase, in addition to all the reference books, were three slim volumes of poetry.

With more than enough to do, he took time off to stare out and up through the open window at the cloudless sky which offered the illusion of peace; work so often battered the romantic side of his nature . . .

A sharp knock on the door jerked him back to the world.

Barnard entered. 'I had word you were trying to get in touch, sir, so since I wasn't far off I decided to come along.'

'Grab a seat.'

Barnard moved a chair from the wall to sit in front of the desk.

'The last of the reports on the scrap depots is through. Nothing.'

'That's a bastard!'

'It is. But we were being optimistic to hope for anything solid. He's smart, so he was always going to make as certain as possible we couldn't trace the Oxford through.'

'At least we can now say we know the method. A car would carry traces that might inculpate him, however well he cleaned it, so it had to be a fresh one each time and afterwards it had to be junked. He bought through small ads, each time looking for a car that had been treated as a classic and not an old banger so that it would have been very well maintained; that he'd have to pay over the odds for such a car was of no account. After the rape, he abandoned it outside the nearest scrap yard which belonged to his company.'

'Does all that supposition take us any closer to being able to arrest him?' Dawes asked wearily.

'At the moment, no, sir.'

'And in the foreseeable future?'

'If we search for past adverts of Oxfords in good condition . . .'

'Just consider the man hours that would call for. And if we found the seller, it's a pound to a penny he'd be unable to make an incriminating identification of the buyer. Even if he did, how would we prove that the Oxford was the one seen by the Potter woman, that Walker-Jones was driving it, and that it was then junked in one of his yards?'

There was a long silence.

Dawes said slowly: 'I've looked at the facts from every possible angle, and some that are probably impossible, and I cannot see how, as things stand, we can hope to find the evidence to charge him.'

'Then we let him get away with rape and murder?'

'A naive question, considering the frequency with which the guilty stay outside, laughing.'

'It's just that . . . Well, it strikes closer to home than usual. It's difficult not to see one's own daughter at risk.'

'Bloody difficult.'

'You know where this leaves us, sir? Our only hope of an arrest is if he rapes, and probably murders, again, and because we now know his identity, we manage to nail him. Because the laws of evidence are pitched to favour the guilty, not establish the truth, we need another victim. Gives a whole new meaning to justice.'

'Explain that to all the modern liberals.'

There was another silence. Dawes again broke it. 'I've had a word with the tame psychiatrist to try to find out if Walker-Jones's knowing he's under suspicion will be enough to stop him raping again. It seems that the increased fear of exposure and arrest may prove stronger than the sexual compulsion; on the other hand, the fact that obviously we cannot find sufficient evidence to arrest him may convince him we never will and this could have the effect of increasing the force of the compulsion.'

'The psychiatrist obviously hasn't a clue. So what's new?'

CHAPTER 21

Walker-Jones stared down at the two accountants' reports
on his desk, unsurprised because they merely confirmed
what was obvious – the financial condition of his companies
was poor. Over the past years of recession, the sales of luxury
cars had plummeted; the cost of recovering scrap metal had
risen as the value of the recovered scrap had dropped; his
foray into the property market had been ill-conceived and
very nearly disastrous. Loans from the banks had had to be
considerably higher than projected, resulting in damagingly
heavy interest payments. But his cocky self-satisfaction –
once a defence against a hostile world, now a part of his
character – made light of the problems. Sales of cars were
picking up, in the scrap world costs had stabilized and values
had risen, and he was out of property. The banks would
reschedule the agreed repayment of loans and within the
year . . .

The intercom buzzed and his secretary said Mr Lynes was
ringing from Renwold.

'Jock here, Mr Walker-Jones.'

He judged Lynes a rogue, but only in a small way and
since he was good at the job, it was worthwhile allowing
him to make a little on the side. 'Yes?'

'I thought you'd want to know the police have been along,
asking did I know you.'

'You told them?'

'Look, Mr W-J, I know how you like things to be played,
but, straight as an arrow, they didn't give me the chance.
Said you owned Jones and Son according to the companies'
register. I'd have looked a right burk to go on saying I didn't
know you.'

132

'What else were they asking?'

'Had you ever turned up in a car for junking, specifically a Morris Oxford. I'd of laughed, only one doesn't laugh when coppers are straight-faced. I said, who's going to bring a Rolls along to be junked?'

'How did they react?'

'Didn't say nothing much, really.'

To foster the impression that the matter was of no account, Walker-Jones changed the conversation and asked about the business.

After ringing off, he telephoned the managers of the other yards. Each one reported a visit from the county police.

He sat back and tried to assess the situation. The police had worked out how he had used old cars in order that they could afterwards be junked without comment. But how had they discovered his ownership of Jones and Son since he'd told them he only owned Royal Motors? They had not questioned the staff on that point – had they done so, he would have been informed – and in any case, the staff did not know about the scrap company. They could have learned nothing from the accountants of Royal Motors because he employed a Gloucester firm for Jones and Son ... They must have learned the truth from an informer. The same one who had previously named him. And as he had so often asked himself, who in the hell could that have been? Until now, he'd decided it must have been someone who'd borne a grudge against him, probably a sacked employee who had denounced him in a spirit of spiteful revenge while ironically believing the charge to be a lie. He'd never really considered an alternative since it was in every man's character to choose to believe whatever was less unwelcome. Yet now, with hindsight, he could appreciate how absurd it had been to accept such an explanation. The odds against a correct identification being made by chance were probably on a par with winning the lottery twice in succession. No, someone very close had twice betrayed him. And who but Serena was in a position to have been able to do so? Yet she had married him for his wealth and would never do anything that could possibly endanger her enjoyment of it, as would his

133

imprisonment. So she could only have betrayed him inadvertently, without realizing the possible consequences . . . He experienced sudden panic. What if the police had also learned that there were times when he made her let him tie her down to the bed? Yet if the police had the slightest intimation of this, surely they would have questioned both him and Serena to discover if it were true? . . . He must discover if his logic were correct, because if Serena had not yet let slip to someone that one of his pleasures could be considered a trifle odd, he must make certain that she never did. How? Get her tight – an easy task – and when her tongue had been loosened, frighten her.

He looked along the dining-room table. 'How about another bottle of wine?'

'Should we, darling?' Serena said, trying not to sound eager.

'Why not?'

'You've always said one bottle between two people is the limit.'

'Rules need to be broken occasionally.' He turned to Pablo. 'Bring up another bottle of Pommard.'

Pablo left.

He watched Serena drain her glass. Left to herself, she'd soon become an alcoholic. Her trouble was, she lacked self-control. 'Did you say you met Lady Wainweather?'

'And had a long chat with her. She was so friendly . . .' She was as big a snob as he, but lacked his ability to hide the fact.

Pablo returned, showed the bottle, refilled their glasses. He picked up the silver serving dishes from the sideboard and presented them.

Twenty-five minutes later, Serena and Walker-Jones went through to the green room.

'How about an Armagnac to aid digestion?' he suggested.

'I really shouldn't have anything more to drink,' she said, slurring a word. 'But if you think it's all right . . .'

Pablo brought in a bottle of Armagnac and two balloon

glasses on a silver salver, put this down on one of the occasional tables, left.

Walker-Jones poured out two generous Armagnacs, handed a glass to her. 'A rather disturbing thing happened today,' he said, as he crossed the floor and sat. 'I had a telephone call from Renwold.'

'Who's that?'

'The scrap yard in the west. The manager told me the police have been there, asking questions about me.'

'Have you been up to something naughty?'

'It seems they still think I might have had something to do with the rapes and murder.'

'Stupid bastards!'

'I'm wondering how they know about Jones and Son since I only told them about Royal Motors.'

'What's it matter?'

'They're suggesting that each time I raped a woman, I took the car I'd used to one of my yards to be junked.'

'Double stupid bastards!'

'The big question is, how did they first learn I own Jones and Son?'

'They know everything about everyone.'

'Did you tell them?'

'What a stupid thing to ask. Stop being so nasty. Serena doesn't like it when her Thomas is nasty to her . . .'

'Did you tell them?'

Warned by his sudden change in manner, she tried to think more clearly. 'Of course I didn't.'

'Have you ever mentioned it to anyone else?'

'Never.'

'Then how did the police learn about it?'

'I don't know.'

'You're lying.'

'No, I'm not; I swear I'm not.' Ironically, that was when she remembered the lunch with Diana and realized that she was lying.

He had not missed her sudden uneasiness. 'You told someone.'

'No,' she answered weakly.

'You know what happens to liars, don't you?'

She knew from experience that when he became really angry, he could lose his self-control. Yet however vehemently she denied the accusation, he was not now going to believe her. 'Sweetie . . .'

'Well?'

'I . . . Maybe I did kind of mention it once. But she knew it was a secret and she'd never have told anyone else, not in a million years.'

'Who?'

'Diana. We had lunch together here one day and . . .'

'You got drunk.'

'It wasn't at all like that and of course I didn't have too much to drink; how can you think I would? I told her how proud of you I am and how successful you are and it just slipped out about the junk yards. She didn't take any notice of what I said. That's exactly how it was, I swear it is.'

Diana. A woman who possessed the rare quality of total loyalty. Simply because he was her brother-in-law, she would refuse even to consider the possibility that he might be the rapist and therefore if she had remembered what Serena had told her she would never have passed on this information to the police, any more than it could have been she who had originally and anonymously named him. But her strength could be her weakness. She would always make the mistake of believing that those close to her enjoyed an equal sense of loyalty. It would not, could not, have occurred to her that her unsuccessful estranged husband would jump at the chance to harm someone who was very, very successful . . . Now he knew how he had been betrayed! But there was one more all-important fact that he did not know. 'What else did you say about me when you had that drunken lunch with Diana?'

'I wasn't even a little bit tiddly . . .'

'What else?' he repeated violently.

'Nothing.'

He stood suddenly, saw her flinch. 'You lied about telling anyone I own Jones and Son.' He crossed to stand in front

136

of her chair. 'You're lying again.' As she pressed back in the chair, scared, he experienced warm pleasure.

'That wasn't a lie. I just forgot I'd told her, that's all.'

'Now you can remember what else you happened to mention.'

'Nothing. I swear it, nothing.'

He gripped her throat, resting his thumbs above her windpipe. 'You did tell her something more, didn't you?'

'No,' she said wildly.

'Keep lying and I'll throttle you.'

'Oh, God, please stop.'

'You told her that sometimes for a laugh I tie you down to the bed.'

He should have remembered something that he had accepted earlier that day – the lesser evil was always chosen. She was certain that if she admitted she'd asked Diana why men did such a thing, he would assume that she'd said that he did. Then his sense of embarrassed humiliation could become so great that he really might throttle her, unaware of what he was doing. 'I swear to God I've never told anyone that, not even Diana.'

Her terror evoked memories. He dropped his hands. 'Upstairs.' His voice was thick.

CHAPTER 22

Adeane stepped out of the car and stood for a moment as he stared at Turnbull Farm in the sunshine. Despite the surrounding estate of modern homes which crowded close, the seventeenth-century farmhouse, no matter how often he saw it, offered a sense of timeless peace which evoked a response in his own mind.

He walked round to the front door and rang the bell. Diana's greeting was antagonistically cold. So much for peaceful sensations! He stepped into the hall. 'I've decided to take Melly to the zoo park unless she's been there recently. Would you know if she has?'

'I've taken her to play with Margaret.'

'Am I early? I thought we'd fixed eleven . . .'

'I wanted her out of the way.' She turned, crossed the hall to the sitting-room. She came to a stop in the centre, her head just clear of the central beam. 'Serena phoned me this morning. She was almost hysterical and part of the time hardly made sense.'

'A not unfamiliar occurrence.'

'Tom's been harassed by the police again because they've learned that he owns the scrap business. He accused Serena of having told them. She said she hadn't, but he wouldn't believe her and in the end she was forced to admit that she'd told me about it over lunch. The next thing was, he was threatening to throttle her because he believed she'd also told me about tying her down to the bed when he bonks her. She was terrified he really would kill her, even if she admitted that all she'd done at another time was ask me why men do that sort of thing, and so she swore blind she'd never mentioned what happened to a living soul. She demanded to know if I'd ever told anyone about it. She was in such a state I decided I had to lie and I said I never had or would ... Do you know something? Until she spoke, it had never occurred to me that I'd breached her confidence by telling you. I'd forgotten that we don't observe the same standards.'

'What are you getting at?'

'Could anything be more obvious? It was you who named Tom to the police.'

'Of course it wasn't.'

'I can remember saying to you how unsurprised you seemed to be to learn the police were questioning him. You betrayed something said to you in the strictest confidence and used it to make a filthy, anonymous accusation. Why? Because you've always hated him ...'

He cut in. 'However I think of him, I wouldn't accuse him like that.'

'Do you really think I lived with you for years without knowing when you're lying? You gave his name to the police. I know that.'

There seemed little point in continuing to deny it. 'All right, I did.'

'You hate him because you're jealous. So when things started going badly wrong for you, your jealousy grew until it turned you rotten.'

'I've only just realized how much you dislike me!'

'I dislike anyone who betrays the trust of friendship.'

'I was faced with either naming him or remaining silent when I knew certain facts which might help the police.'

'You expect me to believe you seriously imagined someone in Tom's position could commit such filthy crimes?'

'Being rich doesn't automatically disqualify him.'

'But in your eyes it automatically qualifies him. I just don't begin to understand how you can have done what you did.'

'Because you don't want to.'

'Having learned the truth, you're right; I don't.'

'If you can manage to become a little less holier-than-thou, take time to ask yourself what you'd have done if you were convinced you might be able to help identify a rapist and murderer; would you really keep silent, knowing the cost of your silence might be more victims?'

'I hope I'd be sufficiently self-honest to identify my motives for what they really were, not try to hide them under the guise of public duty . . . Would you please leave?'

'It'll be a pleasure.' He turned and crossed to the door, came to a stop. He said, without bothering to turn, 'I'll have Melly back by six.'

'I don't want you to see her.'

'You're afraid my complaint's catching?' He faced her. 'Perhaps I need to remind you that she's my daughter as well as yours. I'll pick her up from the Rileys and return her at six.'

'She's not at the Rileys.'

'You said she was with Margaret. If she's not with them, where is she?'

'I have no intention of telling you.'

'You've no right to refuse.'

'I have every right to act in her best interests.'

'Perhaps it's time to start examining your motives, rather than mine. You might learn that you're not defending her, you're using her to hurt me.'

'That's a fool thing to say.'

'Which goes some way to levelling the score.' He left.

As he drove on to the road, he was infuriated to find himself wondering whether his motives in denouncing Walker-Jones had been quite as public spirited as he'd maintained.

Because the wind was from the west, the church bells were just audible through the opened windows of the library. Walker-Jones did not hear them, any more than he saw the beauty of the park. In his mind there was room for only one question. Had Serena been telling the truth when she'd sworn she'd not told Diana about being tied down to the bed? He wanted to believe that she had because then he was certain the police would never amass sufficient evidence to arrest him. But when her fears were not feeding his desires, he could not avoid the question, had she been lying in order

140

to assuage his anger? Her relationship with Diana was not strong because the two sisters had so little in common and normally she would never have indulged in a sensual confidence. But obviously she'd had too much to drink at that luncheon and her tongue had wagged and if she'd told Diana about Jones and Son, she might so easily have spoken also about his funny little habit . . . Yesterday, he'd assured himself that the fact that the police had not questioned him about his sexual habits was proof positive that they did not know about them. Why did not the same reasoning apply today? . . . Of course, she might drunkenly have told Diana, but Diana had decided that this information was too personal to pass on to Adeane, even though she'd mentioned Jones and Son. Alternatively, she'd told Adeane and he'd told the police, but they'd dismissed the information as of no practical relevance. Yet this had to be nonsense. The police must see such information as highly relevant. Then he could return to the certainty that they didn't know. Or could he? Might they not be keeping this knowledge in reserve? If challenged directly, Serena would naturally deny everything. But she was not a strong character and under expert interrogation must break and confess . . . He knew a sense of panic greater than he'd suffered the day before. He could see himself on trial, found guilty, condemned as a murdering pervert, spat on by the mob who were too ignorant to understand . . . Divide and rule. The maxim that had kept rulers on their thrones throughout the millennia. Divide the police from the truth by forcing them to pursue a lie . . .

CHAPTER 23

Adeane checked the time again and his worry grew. Normally, Patricia was back by seven and it was now nearly half past eight. His quick imagination pictured a crash ... He heard the sounds of the front door being opened and hurried out to the hall. 'You're late.'

She looked at her reflection in the mirror above the table before she said: 'I didn't know I had to live by your timetable.'

He was surprised by her aggression. 'It's just that I was becoming worried. Been working late?'

'Do you want an itemized account of my life?'

It was not his day; first Diana, now Patricia. 'All I want right now is your order for drinks.'

'A large whisky.'

As she went into the sitting-room, he made his way to the kitchen where he poured out a whisky and a gin and tonic. He carried the glasses through, handed her one which she accepted without any thanks. He checked the TV programmes, switched the set on. The announcer said that the next programme would be about the secret life of the savannah cheetah.

'You can turn that off,' she said. 'I'm fed up with animals.'

He did so. 'Has it been a very bad day at the office?'

'Why ask?'

'You seem very tired.'

'Who wouldn't be with that bitch riding me all day?'

There were times when he thought it likely that Mary and she gained rather than lost from their fraught relationship.

'All I did this afternoon ...'

Within seconds of her finishing the story, the phone rang.

He stood. 'I'll go.' In the hall, he lifted the receiver. 'Amersford three-seven-one-five-six.'

'Thomas speaking.'

''Evening.' He hoped he didn't sound as surprised as he felt.

'Am I interrupting anything?'

'Nothing of any importance.' Which was as good a description as any of Patricia's bellyaching.

'I'd rather like a word with you tomorrow evening. Would that be convenient?'

'As far as I know, yes.'

'I might have some good news. About seven-thirty, here.'

'Fine.'

'I'll see you tomorrow evening, then.'

As he replaced the receiver, Adeane decided that although a leopard might not be able to change its spots, a Thomas Walker-Jones could occasionally be vaguely friendly.

As he entered the sitting-room, Patricia said: 'Who was it?'

'My brother-in-law, as you prefer me to term him.'

'What on earth does he want?'

'Me to go and see him tomorrow evening.'

'Why?'

'If I'm not letting optimism blind me to his potential for being a shit, either to offer me a job or to tell me about one that he might be able to pull in my favour. Let's be generous and have another drink to celebrate.'

He turned off the road on to the drive and as the view of Farthingstone House widened out, the romantic in him imagined carriages, powdered footmen, crinolines, and whispered confidences behind opened fans. He parked by the side of the central flowerbed, crossed to the portico and rang the bell. He was surprised when the door was opened by Walker-Jones.

'Come along in . . . It's Pablo and Juanita's night off and Serena's with friends, so we're on our own. Good to see you again.'

'It's good to be here,' Adeane replied, not to be outshone in insincerities.

'I thought we'd have a chat and a drink in the green room. I always think that at this time of the evening it's the nicest room; a very good view of the park. Nothing as beautiful as the English countryside on a fine summer's day, is there?'

'Nothing.' Any moment now, would the other launch into '. . . In some melodious plot of beeches green, and shadows numberless . . .'?

They entered the green room, very bright because a shaft of late sunlight cut across the centre of it.

'Sit you down, Richard. And will you risk trying a margarita?'

'To risk is to live,' he answered as he sat on the nearest armchair.

'I've never mixed one before, but I've always wanted to and Serena saw limes for sale in Harrods and brought me back a couple of pounds – or should I say a kilo?'

'Pounds sound more plentiful.'

'Imagine living under a government so weak it throws away avoirdupois for metric, merely to cuddle up to the Continentals. Did not God give us the English Channel to separate us from them?'

'It seems the most logical reason.'

'I'll go and squeeze the limes. Everything else is ready so it won't take me a second.' He hurried out of the room.

Adeane settled back in the chair. He thought that Diana would appreciate it if he rang her the next morning and asked her whether she knew if Tom's sudden friendliness meant he was just back from Damascus . . . He remembered that any call from him would be ill received by her.

Walker-Jones returned with two large crystal glasses. As he handed one to Adeane, he said: 'It looks rather a lot, but I thought it would save my having to go out again if I served the two halves together.' He raised his glass. 'Your health.'

'And yours.' It was far from the best margarita Adeane had drunk. Indeed, on the second tasting he decided it was the worst. It pricked his tongue, as hot curry would, and there was a metallic taste as if it had been mixed in a shaker not properly cleaned after being polished.

'Well, what's the verdict?'

'As good as expected.'

'Excellent, excellent! . . . Now, I had hoped to be able to give you definite news, but unfortunately, I can't. Still, there's every reason to think it won't be very long before I can.'

'News about what?'

'I was having lunch with an old friend who's chairman of a large company and he mentioned, en passant, that the firm's PRO is about to retire and none of his juniors is considered up to his job. The firm's engaged an agency to find a replacement, but so far all the people sent along for interviews have proved to be wanting too much and offering too little. The curse of the age, wouldn't you agree?'

'Rather depends on which side of the fence one's standing.'

'Indeed. A good point.' He drank. 'Naturally, when I heard this, I thought of you.'

Adeane wanted to speak, but he suddenly felt as if his mouth were so filled with cotton wool he could not. Then the sensation vanished. 'That was very kind of you.'

'Where's the point in being a relative – even if only by marriage – if one doesn't seize the chance to help out when one can?'

The cotton wool returned, drying out his mouth. He drank eagerly.

'Naturally, I spoke about you to my friend and said how good at your work you were.'

'That was very . . .' He couldn't finish. Walker-Jones's face seemed to swell, then it became covered in a grating of lines that shimmered. He knew a fast-growing sense of an approaching, but unspecified, threat.

'I suggested he interviewed you as soon as possible and I thought he'd agreed, but then he rang to say he'd have to leave everything in the hands of the personnel manager because that's the way it's supposed to be done. Big firms are becoming increasingly bureaucratic. But at least he will strongly suggest you are called for an interview and unless the personnel manager is a fool, he'll accept the suggestion. Of course, from then on it's all up to you, but there can't be any doubt that when they've talked to you and learned about your experience, they'll offer the job.'

He was being drawn with ever-increasing speed into a black, bottomless hole.

'Are you feeling all right, Richard? Is something the matter?'

He struggled to answer, to call for help, but the black hole engulfed him.

He awoke and was violently sick.

He lay, unable to find the energy to move, even though the position in which he found himself was extremely uncomfortable. He tried to make sense of the world, but couldn't; his head was pounding to the blows of a blacksmith's Goliath hammer, his mouth tasted as if it had been filled with the contents of someone's dustbin, and his stomach was threatening further revolt.

Time passed. He struggled into an upright position and found he was in the front of his car. Looking through the windscreen, he could see a clump of high bushes that were outlined by the soft moonlight and as he watched he saw the loom of moving headlights beyond the bushes and heard the rising and falling note of a passing car.

He tried to forget his physical suffering and look back in time to discover what had happened. Memory arrived in snippets. Driving up to Farthingstone House; Thomas in a strangely affable mood; the mention of a possible job; a drink the size of an Irishman's pint, that had tasted distinctly odd; a growing disorientation that had been like, yet unlike and far more abrupt than, the onset of drunkenness . . .

It was a long, long time since he'd drunk himself insensible. Had he made a fool of himself at the house? Only time would tell. Correction. If he had, Tom would very soon let him know and he could kiss the job goodbye. No one wanted a drunken PRO; there were far too many of them around already . . . He couldn't remember leaving the house, but then loss of memory was part and parcel of drunkenness.

Obviously, he had headed for home but collapsed on the way. And somehow – so far, anyway – had escaped the attention of the police. So now he had to discover where he was and continue the journey, driving like Agag . . .

The moonlight was not strong enough for him to recognize his surroundings and he switched on the headlights. He was parked in a short, sharply curving stretch of road which he didn't recognize. Then he remembered the car which had passed earlier and he decided he was in a lay-by, probably formed when the road had been straightened. There was, however, no such lay-by on the route home.

He started the engine, engaged first gear, and let out the clutch. The car jerked and stalled. He repeated the sequence; same result. Only then did he remember to release the handbrake. He went very slowly around the sharp bend to come to a *Stop* sign. He drew out, turned left, and within a couple of hundred yards identified where he was by a long, centuries-old barn, set back. Four Oaks crossroads lay just ahead. He marvelled at the instinct of self-preservation which had overcome his drunkenness sufficiently to persuade him into the lay-by. Had he carried on along the road, he would have ended up in Beechtown and must surely have been nobbled by the police.

Twenty minutes later, he let himself into the house. Halfway along the upstairs corridor, his right foot decided to go independent and caused him to lose his balance and crash to the floor.

There was a muffled call from the bedroom. 'Is that you?'

If it wasn't, she was in for a nasty shock. As he struggled to his feet, Patricia opened the bedroom door.

'Where have you been? God, you're a sight! You've been sick down yourself. You're drunk! Well, you're not sleeping in my room when you're like that. You can use the other bedroom and if you make a mess, you'll clear it up.' She returned into the bedroom and slammed the door shut.

It was a good job he hadn't hoped for sympathy.

CHAPTER 24

Eason heard the DI arrive and he left his room, went down the corridor to the next one, knocked and entered.

''Morning, Vaughan,' Barnard said, as he sat behind the desk.

Christian names were a certain sign that the DI was in a cheerful mood. Not for long, Eason thought.

'Let's have the list, then.'

He passed across the desk the list of incidents – not necessarily identified as crimes – that had been reported during the night.

'Anything on the missing girl?'

'Nothing fresh. She left the stables where she keeps her horse at livery soon after dark. She was on a Vespa and the journey should have taken twenty minutes. She lives with her parents and it was her father reported her missing just before midnight. There is a boyfriend and I've detailed Bissell to have a word with him.'

'Might not be looking too good.'

'I'm afraid not.'

'I hope it's ridiculous to suggest that that bastard is giving us the two-fingers sign?'

'I've been wondering.'

'Sounds crazy to suggest a man would rape and murder as much to show his contempt for us as to assuage his perverted desires. Only we are dealing with a mind that's part crazy, part smart ... Better ten guilty men go free than one innocent man be found guilty. Tell that to her parents if it turns out she's been raped and murdered and we haven't pulled the bastard in solely because we can't find sufficient evidence for the courts.'

*   *   *

Adeane awoke and wished he hadn't; death would have had no sting, grave, no victory. Lump together every hangover he had ever suffered in the past and it could only be a pale shadow of the one he was now suffering. That margarita must have been made from diesel oil, not tequila . . .

He slept.

He awoke and life was more approachable. The curtains had not been drawn and the room was sunny, forcing him to squint as he raised his left wrist to look at his watch. As he did so, he noticed two scratches on the back of his hand – how he'd suffered them was just one more thing of which he had no memory. The time was a quarter to twelve.

He bathed, looked out clean clothes, and went downstairs. Shuddering at the thought of anything to eat, he made himself coffee. As he drank, he tried to decide whether to assume he'd made an exhibition of himself the previous night and to ring Tom, swallow all pride, and apologize with slavish humility, banking that by massaging the other's ego he'd head off rejection, or to remain silent, hoping against hope that he'd not made too gross a fool of himself whilst still at the house . . . If only he could remember something about his departure. But it remained a complete blank . . . Slavishly servile apologies reminded him of Patricia. How to overcome her resentment? Flowers? She gave them small count. Perfume? He could afford only the smallest possible quantity and size was always important to her. Chocolates? Bought from the shop that imported them direct from Belgium and packed them so extravagantly that a one-pound box looked like a two-pound one?

He finished the coffee, put the mug on the draining-board, checked doors were locked and windows shut, left the house. No walking for him today and he'd go by car. Which was when he realized he'd no recollection of where he'd parked. He visually searched the road and because so many cars were away at the owners' workplaces, he was able to see the dark-green 205, almost at the end of the road.

He was within twenty feet of the Peugeot, which he was approaching from behind, before he noticed that the right-hand rear light pod was smashed. He came to a sudden stop, scared by the thought that he'd been involved in a crash. But if that were so, it was almost inevitable that he'd have regained consciousness in a police cell, not in the lay-by. He must have backed into something, somewhere. He resumed walking. He hoped he hadn't caused too much damage.

The police normally investigated the disappearance of a person only after time had passed, because experience showed that despite the panicky fears of relatives and friends, almost all such disappearances were not evidence of tragedy, but of thoughtlessness or even malicious intent to alarm. But Barnard ordered an initial search to be made immediately along the route Wendy Marshall would have taken to return home.

When little more than a mile from Wendy's house, a PC saw a Vespa in the shallow ditch which divided the grass verge from woods. He approached no closer than was necessary to read the rear numberplate, used his mobile to relay the information. After a brief pause, he was called back to be told that other searchers were being directed to the woods and they were to make certain no one entered them or approached the Vespa. The detective inspector would be out as soon as possible.

Barnard braked the CID Escort to a halt a hundred yards back from the first string of police tape. He and Eason left the car, acknowledged the greeting of a PC, walked along the road until immediately above the Vespa. Because the grass and weeds were long, only parts of it were clearly visible; parts that varied very slightly as the breeze moved the foliage. They ducked under the tape and, marking their route, stepped down into the ditch. There were signs of damage to the handlebars and the seat.

They returned to the road. Barnard asked the nearest PC if anyone present knew the neighbourhood and the PC shouted out the question to another man who, in turn, passed it on. After a couple of minutes, a PC who had been keeping watch in a field hurried up to them. The woods, he said, were roughly fifty acres in size and belonged to the farmer whose land ringed them; officially called Colling Wood, they were known locally as Willie's Wood because the owner's Christian name was William and many of the local babies had been conceived in them.

'Are there rides?' Barnard asked.

'There's a main one right through, sir, and a couple of smaller ones on either side of that.'

'Where does this main ride meet the road?'

'Fifty yards further up from here.'

Barnard led the way along to a five-bar gate. After a quick, yet thorough, examination of both gate and uprights, Eason secured it fully open with a rock. The ride was on average ten feet wide and the patches of sparse grass that grew along it bore all the signs of being frequently crushed by passing cars; the clay soil was rock hard and obviously incapable of taking impressions. On either side there was a typical jumble of ash, hornbeam, chestnut, birch, and occasional oak. As they walked, pigeons frequently rose with clapping wings and flew away.

When level with the first ride off to the left, Eason said: 'There's something.'

Barnard, who'd been walking on the right-hand side, crossed. Around the base of several ash trunks which had grown from a pollarded bole there was a scattering of glass or plastic slivers, some red, some plain; the bark of one of the trunks bore a slight gash which was white enough to show the damage was recent. 'Rear light pod of a car?'

'Could be. If this is a lovers' lane, like the PC was suggesting, there'll be plenty of traffic at night.'

Barnard studied the area. If a car had driven into the woods and later wanted to return to the road, it was probable the driver would back into the side ride to make the turn. He would not have to misjudge by much to miss centring the ride and hit the trunk . . . There was nothing to indicate that had the car turned there and hit the tree, it had any connection with the missing woman, but any police officer developed an instinct, probably more often right than wrong, and his was telling him that it did. 'I'm going to call up a full search of the woods,' he said harshly.

The searchers kept as close together as their numbers allowed and maintained a reasonably straight line, despite all the minor detours which individually had to be made, working to a compass heading. Twenty-five minutes after they'd entered from the road, a call brought everyone to a halt. Barnard hurried over to the right flank, swearing when his feet became briefly entangled in undergrowth.

'Over there, sir,' said a PC, his open-neck shirt stained with sweat. 'A female body.'

'Have you moved?'

'Come back a couple of paces.'

The reaction of so many; the instinctive attempt to escape the inescapable. Barnard had a battered haversack over one shoulder and from this he brought out a handful of small red flags, mounted on metal shafts. He used these to mark each step he took.

She lay in a clump of brambles that grew in the centre of a small clearing. She was naked and on her back, hands behind her, legs apart. She had been blindfolded and gagged with masking tape that, at least from a distance of six feet, looked exactly similar to the tape used on other victims. Flies were settling on her, particularly around the eyes.

Familiarity never lessened the impact of brutal death.

On her return home, Adeane met Patricia in the hall. He held up the box of chocolates which had been wrapped in elaborately decorated paper and tied in a fanciful bow with thin gold-coloured string. 'Forgive?'

'You were disgustingly drunk.'

'*Mea maxima maxima culpa.* And to express my deepest, humblest, most abject apologies, I offer you these, each a prayer for melting forgiveness.'

'You just think it's funny, don't you?'

'Far from it.'

'Then why talk such balls?'

'It's my way of trying to cover my embarrassment.'

'You frightened me silly. And you were in a disgusting state . . . Did you get drunk there?'

'To tell the truth, I'm not sure.'

'If you can't remember, you must have done. He's really going to want to help you find a job now, isn't he?'

'I can only hope that beneath the arctic exterior there beats a tropical heart.'

'That's right, keep on laughing.'

'My embarrassment remains.' He held out the chocolates. 'Please. In the names of the three daughters of Zeus.'

'What's in it?'

'Chocolates.'

'Soft or hard centres?'

'Truffles from Edwina. The *crème de la crème*.'

She took the parcel.

'"To err is human, to forgive, divine."'

'I'm not divine,' she snapped, only appreciating the ambiguity of that after she'd spoken. 'You really think I'm going to forgive you behaving like a complete swine just because you give me some chocolates?'

He'd known he was going to find the going hard, but had hoped, not this hard.

On the nine o'clock news, Wendy Marshall's death was reported in greater detail than on previous bulletins and part of the initial press conference was shown. In this excerpt, the assistant chief constable (crime) was shown refusing to speculate whether this murder had been carried out by the serial rapist; repeatedly, he stated that the evidence had yet to be properly evaluated and until it was, it would be impossible to judge. Crime scenes followed – policemen stolidly standing guard, long lengths of police tape billowing in the breeze, trees, the comings and goings of unidentified people – to the accompaniment of a voice-over which claimed that despite the official statement, the police were in fact conducting the investigation from the viewpoint that the murderer was the serial rapist who had also killed Jane Rowland.

*   *   *

Walker-Jones switched off the television. 'I suppose you realize what this is going to mean to us?'

'Why should it mean anything?' Serena said.

He admired her ability not to understand what she did not wish to understand. 'The police consider me to be a suspect in the other murder and the rapes and . . .'

'You must make them stop being so ridiculous.'

'. . . and since this murder was so close to here, inevitably their suspicions will be increased and they'll be bothering me once more.'

'They've no right to behave like the Gestapo.'

'Unfortunately, so far they've stayed within their rights. For my part, I'll have the right to refuse to answer any question, but because they are not chosen for their intelligence, their reactions are totally predictable – they'll treat silence as a sign of guilt. Therefore, if I'm to end this bother, it's in my interest not to insist on my rights, but to cooperate; to answer all their questions. Which means we need to discuss something. They'll want to know where I was at the time of the woman's death.'

'Then you can tell them you were here.'

'Quite. Only they'll demand proof of that and as I was on my own because Pablo and Juanita had the evening off and you were with Sylvia and Basil, I won't be able to provide it.'

'I said you should have come with me.'

'And as I explained, I couldn't because of work that turned up at the last moment and had to be dealt with immediately.'

'But if you had, there'd be no bother now.'

'With hindsight, everything is possible. As things are, however, if I can't corroborate my evidence, the police are going to disbelieve me and do their damnedest to prove I'm guilty. If necessary, they'll even twist the evidence to that end.'

'They'd never do anything like that.'

'They'll do whatever they want, just so long as they reckon not to be found out.' He rose, walked over to the fireplace and stood with his back to it. 'We have to face the fact that I'm likely to be in danger of being arrested for murder and rape. I doubt I have to spell out exactly what that could mean for us. People rush to believe their friends and acquaintances are in trouble, especially when they've reason to envy them; people will say that even though I'm exonerated, where there's smoke, there's fire; I only got off because there wasn't the evidence to find me guilty. Some people we know might remain friendly, but most wouldn't; we'd face more closed doors than open ones.'

'They couldn't be so beastly,' she said shrilly, aghast at the thought of social ostracism.

'I'm afraid that's how it's going to be. Unless . . .'

'Unless what?'

'We can prevent any chance of my being accused by proving it was impossible I could have killed the woman because I was here, at home.'

'But . . . but haven't you just been saying you can't?'

'On my own, no; but with your help, I can.'

'What d'you mean?'

'If you tell the police that you returned here just before ten, you give me a complete alibi.'

'But it was almost one in the morning because those friends of Sylvia were such fun and you'd told me not to rush home and . . .'

'There's no need for the police to be told any more than that you went up to London and were back here by ten o'clock.'

'You're asking me to lie?'

'To change the facts slightly because it will be both in our interests and the interests of the police since it will stop them continuing to waste their time by believing me to be a possible suspect. If you tell them you visited friends, they'll demand to know their names and then they'll question Sylvia and Basil, who are bound to say you did not leave their place until after midnight. However, say you went up to London to shop and go to a cinema and you will leave them with no way of disproving your word.'

'I . . . I don't think I can do that.'

'Why not?'

'I'd be so scared. It's such a terribly serious case . . .'

'You'd rather see me arrested and charged with murder; you'd rather our lives are ruined?'

'Of course I wouldn't. But . . . it's just . . .'

'Then when you're questioned, you'll tell the police what I've just said. Adding that we went to bed after midnight, but nothing more.'

'But there'd be such awful trouble if they found out I was lying.'

He had been prepared for her to refuse. Someone as selfish and self-centred as she would always have greater regard for her own position than anyone else's. 'Perhaps you need to understand something, my dear. The recession has hit all businesses, but mine more than most; luxury cars haven't been selling and scrap metal has been in oversupply. The companies have been running at a loss and some time ago I had to ask the banks for loans, secured on assets. Profits have not been restored as quickly as projected and recently I've had to return to the banks to ask for the loans to be rescheduled. They were very reluctant to agree and it was only with the greatest difficulty that I persuaded them to do so.'

'I never knew all this.'

'There was no need for you to do so. However, now there is. Thanks to a lot of hard work and an upturn in the economy, we are returning to good profitability and within a reasonable period, everything should be sorted out. But if I publicly come under suspicion of murder and rape, inevitably, human nature being what it is, customers will boycott my companies, full profitability will not be regained, and the banks will take fright. This will have a catastrophic effect. In order to satisfy their demands, I had to include this estate as security. So if the police are not persuaded that I cannot be the rapist and murderer, they'll arrest me, which must mean that we will lose everything we now possess, including this house.'

Detective Chief Superintendent Dawes stood by the window of Barnard's office, looking out across the road at the vicarage. 'Let's have a run-through.'

Barnard, seated at his desk, said: 'The pathologist times death at between ten and midnight, with the usual reservation that the times aren't sacrosanct. The victim was manually throttled after having been raped repeatedly. There was no semen. There were traces of bloodied skin under one of her nails which suggests she managed to fight and scratch her assailant before her hands were secured; four loose pubic hairs were recovered and these are almost certainly foreign, though tests will be needed before we can be certain.

'There was bruising on her shoulder and thigh which corresponds with the damage to the jacket and jeans she was wearing. Remembering the Vespa was damaged, it seems probable she sustained the bruising by falling off that. There's been no sign of the dog.'

'Any contact traces on the Vespa?'

'None. So it doesn't seem she was knocked off with a car. So either she skidded and fell and the murderer happened to come across her before she had remounted, or he cut in ahead of her and frightened her to the point where she lost control. The odds against the first make it virtually certain it was the second. Apart from the slivers of what we're assuming was a rear-light pod, no traces have been found in the woods; the ground was far too hard to take any impressions.'

'At this stage, there's nothing to tie the slivers in with the murderer's car, is there?'

'Nothing. Which means the odds have to be that they're from some other car.'

'But I take it you've notified all garages and retailers and asked for information on anyone who needs a new rear-light pod?'

'Yes, sir.'

'Anything more?'

'On the face of things, only that the masking tape is similar to what's been used before.'

'Making it virtually certain it's the same man, since his method was on all fours with past cases.'

'Yes. The only thing is . . .'

'Well?'

'Three things puzzle me. Why has the murderer left so many traces this time when previously there have been none?'

'Carelessness.'

'But he's previously planned and executed his rapes and murder with meticulous care.'

'If criminals were always as careful as they intended to be, we'd only catch the half-witted. What's your second problem?'

'Why choose a victim this close to home?'

'Sudden opportunity provided a temptation he couldn't resist. And the last puzzle?'

'Why go for so different a method of finding the victim when the previous method has always worked so successfully; this time, things could have so easily gone badly wrong?'

'Do you have an answer?'

'A theory. Something has happened that has caused him to rush into action without taking the time to plan and he was driving around in his own car.'

'Can you put a name to the "something"?'

'No, I can't.'

'Then it doesn't take us anywhere.'

'I did say it was only a theory.'

'I prefer facts.'

'So do I, sir. But where are they?'

'We'd better go and find out.'

They were driven the three-quarters of a mile – longer

than the actual distance because of one-way roads – from divisional HQ to the showrooms of Royal Motors by a uniform PC. One of the salesmen directed them upstairs where Miss Purvis met them and showed them into the chairman's office.

Walker-Jones did not bother to stand. 'I can give you ten minutes only,' he said curtly.

Dawes, refusing to take offence at the reception, said pleasantly: 'I'm sure that'll be plenty time enough to let us cover the ground . . . May we sit?' Without waiting for an answer, he and Barnard moved chairs away from the wall, set them before the desk, and sat, in a show of confidence that was designed to gain the psychological high ground. 'We're making inquiries concerning the death of Miss Wendy Marshall and wonder if you can help us in the matter.'

'Why do you think I might be able to?'

'The evidence to date suggests that her murderer was the same man who murdered Miss Rowland and raped several other women.'

'Have you come here to repeat the slanderous accusations you made previously? If so, I've nothing more to say unless Mr Belling is also present.'

'I don't think we need cause you that expense which would, no doubt, be considerable. Let me assure you, Mr Walker-Jones, we're not here to make any accusation whatsoever; merely to ask if you know anything regarding Miss Marshall's death which might help us in identifying the murderer.'

'I do not.'

'Then we have only one more question. Where were you on Monday evening?'

Walker-Jones reached across the desk for the nearer phone. 'I am going to call Mr Belling.'

'Hang on, there's nothing personal in that question. Already today we've asked five other people, none of whom can be considered a suspect. All we're trying to do is build up a picture of that night. Asking you where you were carries no inference whatsoever.'

After an initial hesitation, he withdrew his hand.

'So if you'd just like to answer?'

'I was at home.'

'All the evening?'

'Yes.'

'Were there others present?'

'My brother-in-law was there for a while.'

'Your brother-in-law being Mr Adeane?'

'Yes.'

'Can you say roughly when he arrived and when he left?'

'He turned up on time, at seven-thirty. I suppose he stayed for about half an hour.'

'And your wife was there?'

'She was out.'

'When did she return?'

'Just before ten.'

'You obviously keep a careful note of times.'

'It so happens that she arrived home in time to watch the ten o'clock news.'

'Then that's just about as certain as it could be ... Were the servants in the house?'

'It was their night off.'

'Then you were on your own from about eight until a little before ten?'

'Yes.'

'Did your wife remain in the house after she returned?'

'Would you expect her to leave at that time of night?'

'Forgive me, but we do have to be pedantically precise. You're saying that she remained at home with you?'

'Yes.'

'Have you any objection to our asking her to confirm that?'

'I am not used to being called a liar.'

'We have no intention of doing any such thing. It's just that we always try to corroborate evidence, even when we can be perfectly satisfied that it's correct. People usually understand.'

'Very well. But I insist on being present when you speak to her.'

'We'd expect you to be. When and where would be most convenient to you both?'

Walker-Jones checked his appointments diary at some length. 'I could just manage six-thirty at my house.'

'Thanks very much. Then we look forward to seeing you later on.' Dawes led the way out of the room.

Ignoring solid yellow lines, the PC had remained parked immediately in front of the showrooms and they had merely to cross the pavement and climb into the back of the car.

'What's your verdict?' Dawes asked, as they settled.

'I don't think I'd buy a second-hand car from you,' Barnard replied, hoping the other would have the sense of humour to accept that as a compliment.

It had been estimated by a disgruntled sergeant that by the time an accused was brought to trial, up to fifty-three forms might have to be filled in, signed, and countersigned; Barnard, faced with a mountain of paperwork because he'd been in the field for much of the past days, would have put the total very much higher.

Eason entered and stared at the many files. 'Are you having fun, guv?'

'Any more comments and you're drafted in to help.'

'I'd rather not. Molly says that if I don't start spending a bit more time at home, she'll think I'm a lodger . . . I've just been buzzed by Lexington Garages. They've had a Peugeot 205 come in for a new rear-light pod.'

'Not a Rolls or a Volvo? Ah, well, they're always quick to tell us we can't win 'em all. A couple out for a bonk had a minor bang as well.'

'Hang on. The owner's name and address is Adeane, seventeen, Rander's Road, East Amersford.'

'This,' Barnard said slowly, 'I did not expect.'

They sat in the sitting-room, Barnard and Eason on the settee, Adeane in one of the armchairs. The window was open and from time to time the sounds of passing traffic made them raise their voices.

'Mr Walker-Jones estimates you left Farthingstone House at around eight,' Barnard said. 'Would you agree with that?'

'Without being at all certain, I'd have thought it was a little later,' Adeane replied. They had explained their reason for questioning him in such vague terms that their explanation had told him nothing. He presumed, with a sinking feeling, that he'd been wrong to hope he'd get away with driving when too drunk to remember anything; someone had noted the number of his car and reported it.

'And having left his house, you returned here?'

'That's right.'

'Did you drive directly here?'

About to answer in the affirmative, he remembered that the lay-by near Four Oaks crossroads was not on the route he would have taken if he had made straight for home. 'No. It was such a fine night, I decided to have a bit of a wander around.'

'Was it an incident-free drive?'

'Yes, of course.'

'Then you didn't suffer any accident?'

'No.'

'Then how did you manage to smash the rear-light pod of your car?'

Burns had said it so much more succinctly than ever he could; one little lie and he'd shunted himself into a morass. 'How d'you know about that?' he asked, playing for time in order to work out some way in which to make out he was not the liar he was.

'Your garage reported it to us.'

'Why should they do that?'

'We'd asked them, and others, to report the replacement sale of a rear-light pod ... Would you like to say how it became smashed, if not on your journey back?'

He had thought up the obvious answer. 'I've no garage so the car has to be left in the road. Someone parking behind went too close and then forgot to leave a name and address. That happens all the time.'

Barnard's expression gave no hint as to whether he believed or disbelieved what he'd just been told. 'Where did you drive on Monday night, after leaving Farthingstone House?'

'I thought I'd answered that.'

'Only very vaguely.'

'Because I drove just for pleasure. The night was fine and in the countryside the traffic was thin.'

'You don't wish to be more specific?'

'Like the young lady locked into a chastity belt, if I could, I would, but I can't.'

'You can, though, say whether or not you drove into Colling Wood.'

'Colling Wood ... Isn't that where the poor girl was murdered?'

'It is.'

'For God's sake, you're not suggesting I know anything about that?'

'On the ride leading up to where her body was found there were a number of slivers from a rear-light pod and it's clear these came from a car that was backing to turn and drive on to the road. The woods are known locally as a lovers' lane and so quite a few cars will enter them. What we're trying to do now is determine whether the car whose lights were smashed was one of these, or whether it was being driven by the murderer.'

'I've never been near the woods. I don't even know exactly

where they are. I've told you, the lights were bust when the car was parked outside.'

Eason said: 'I had a word with the mechanic who mended your car. You told him you'd no idea how the pod got broken.'

'He's one hell of a talker and I was trying to keep the conversation short.'

Barnard said: 'You've scratched your hand.'

Adeane looked down. 'What if I have?'

'How did that happen?'

'I've no idea.'

'You seem to be somewhat unobservant.'

'Haven't you ever scratched yourself and not known how or when? I expect it was gardening.'

'The dead woman had bloodied skin under one of her nails. This suggests she struggled with her assailant before her hands were secured behind her back.'

'Christ! You're not suggesting, you're accusing!'

'At this stage, I'm merely wondering why you are repeatedly lying.'

'You admitted you didn't know what car went into the woods and smashed its rear lights, now you're saying it was mine because I've scratched my hand . . .'

'Mr Adeane, before you go any further, consider this. Forensic scientists can usually match substances and the garage has handed us the remains of the light pod from your car; these days the scientists with DNA testing can match human traces such as blood and flesh virtually beyond question to an individual. If these slivers are from your car and the flesh under the dead woman's fingernails was from your hand, we are going to be able to prove this. If you are totally innocent of Wendy Marshall's rape and death, surely it's obvious that your best way of establishing this is to tell us the truth now, not continue to lie.'

Adeane knew panicky desperation. When he'd been convinced they were trying to find out if he'd had an accident when drunk in charge, it had seemed reasonable to lie to try to escape the consequences, yet now to go on lying must place him in danger of being thought guilty of rape and murder. To prevent the absurdity of that, he must now tell the truth. 'What really happened was, I was too tight to remember.'

'Would you explain that.'

'When I was at my brother-in-law's, he offered me a drink; elephant size and it tasted awful. But I wasn't going to tell him that and I drank it and blacked out.'

'Like that?'

'Just like that.'

'Where were you when you came to?'

'In my car in the Four Oaks lay-by. I was feeling like I'd died the week before, but I managed to drive back here.'

'Are you saying you have no recollection of what happened between blacking out in Farthingstone House and coming to in the lay-by?'

'Yes.'

'What was the time when you regained consciousness?'

'The last thing I was bothered about was what the time was.'

'Do you know when you arrived home?'

'No.'

'Would your wife know?'

'My girlfriend. I've no idea if she would.'

'Where were you on the night of the first of this month?'

'What's that to do with anything?'

'That was when Jane Rowland was murdered.'

'I was here, at home.'

'Where were you on the twenty-second of last month?'

'Can't you understand? I don't know anything about the murders and rapes.'

'Then you can't have any reason for not telling us where you were.'

'I've a very good reason. I can't remember.'

'You weren't here?'

'I almost definitely was, but how the hell am I supposed to be certain where I was on one particular night a month ago?'

Barnard stood. 'We'll probably have some more questions

to ask you later on, so I hope you'll be around to answer them.'

'Is that a threat?'

'A friendly comment.'

'Needed because you're so used to disbelieving people, you can't understand I'm telling the truth now. I wasn't anywhere near Colling Wood.'

'How can you be that definite when you've told us you remember nothing between drinking at Farthingstone House and coming to in the lay-by?'

'You think I could rape her when I was blind? Hasn't anyone ever told you that when one's drunk, one can't find any lead in the pencil?'

'There's an exception to every rule, even that one. And for the moment we only have your word that you were so drunk.'

'Ask Mr Walker-Jones.'

'We intend to.'

It was bitterly ironic that whereas he had been hoping against hope that Thomas had not thought him drunk, now he had to hope ever more fervently that the other would agree that he had been so drunk that even the sight of Venus arising from the sea would have left him unmoved.

CHAPTER 27

Neither Dawes nor Barnard was surprised to find Belling, as well as Walker-Jones and his wife, in the green room at Farthingstone House. Belling was aggressively brusque. 'What is your reason for wishing to question Mrs Walker-Jones?'

'To ask her whether she can corroborate what her husband has told us,' Dawes replied.

'Why should his evidence require corroboration?'

'I'm sure you appreciate that the value of corroborative evidence is as great to the innocent as the guilty.'

Belling, usurping Walker-Jones's preferred position in front of the fireplace, looked annoyed.

Barnard turned to Serena, who sat on the settee. 'Would you be kind enough to tell us where you were on Monday evening?'

She answered nervously and so quickly her listeners had difficulty in hearing her. 'Here, after I got back from London.'

'When did you go up there?'

'I caught the two o'clock train.'

She was wearing what even to Barnard's fashion-ignorant eyes was more a creation than a dress; pinned on her breast was a brooch with a central diamond that sparkled ice fire as she moved. Money could buy anything, he thought; it could buy an unprepossessing, balding, bellied man a beautiful woman half his age. 'And when did you return?'

'On the eight-twenty.'

'What did you do in London?'

'I did some shopping and went to the cinema.'

'Do you think you spoke to anyone who will remember you?'

'Hardly a relevant question,' Belling said.

Dawes contradicted him. 'On the contrary. Such a person would be able to corroborate time and place and, as I think we've agreed, that would be of help to Mrs Walker-Jones.'

'She has no need of such help.'

Barnard resumed the questioning at a sign from Dawes. 'If you caught the eight-twenty, you were back here by when, Mrs Walker-Jones?'

'Just before ten.'

'You can be sure of that?'

'Do you wish to challenge the statement?' Belling demanded.

'I was just wondering if the time could be fixed by some definite event.'

'As a matter of fact,' she said, 'we watched the ten o'clock news. Does that help?'

'It provides definitive evidence,' said Belling.

'What did you do after watching the news?' Barnard asked.

'We saw a couple more programmes before going to bed.'

'Can you say what time that was?'

'Not really, except it was after midnight.'

'Thank you.'

'Is that all?' said Belling.

'All that I have to ask Mrs Walker-Jones, but there is something more I'd like to clear up with the help of her husband.'

'What?'

Barnard, ignoring the question, faced Walker-Jones. 'You told us before that Mr Adeane was here on Monday evening.'

'Well?' Walker-Jones's antagonism was the equal of, if not more than, Belling's.

'Whilst he was here, did you offer him a drink?'

'Naturally.'

'How many drinks did he have?'

'When I know someone has to drive, I never offer more than one.'

'In what state would you judge he was in when he left here?'

'I don't understand the question.'

'Was he sober?'

'Of course.'

'He had no trouble in speaking; he was in complete control of his movements?'

Belling said: 'Precisely what is the purpose of this line of questioning?'

Dawes stood. 'We don't need to bother you any longer. Thank you for your kind cooperation.' He sounded as if his thanks were genuine.

Barnard settled behind the wheel of the CID Escort, swore.

'Something bothering you?' Dawes asked with heavy irony.

'I feel like a puppy at the end of a leash. We're being led along, so bloody smoothly there's nothing we can do but follow.'

'Until we decide it's time to stop and snarl.'

'Are we ever going to be in a position to do that?'

'Sooner or later.'

'I hope you're right, sir. Only the omens aren't good. He's committed at least five rapes and two murders and we can't begin to land him. In fact, just the opposite. He's forcing us to waste time pursuing an innocent man.'

'You know what usually defeats a clever man? Sooner or later, he becomes so clever he confuses even himself.'

'That'll be a change from him confusing us.'

They were watching television when the front door bell rang. Adeane stood, went through to the hall and opened the front door. 'What the hell is it this time?' he asked as he faced Barnard and Eason.

'One or two more questions,' Barnard answered. 'We need to check out something Mr Walker-Jones has told us.'

'Double-check everything he tells you.'

Patricia stepped into the hall and stared curiously at the two detectives. Adeane introduced them, then said: 'We might as well go into the other room and sit.'

'There's no need to disturb you to that extent. We can ask our questions quickly and then leave you unharassed.' Barnard's manner was not unfriendly. 'In what state were you when you left Farthingstone House on Monday evening?'

'I told you.'

'You might like to alter what you said then.'

'And I might not.'

'Mr Walker-Jones says that when you left his house at around eight that evening you were completely sober.'

'What's going on?' Patricia asked.

Barnard turned to face her. 'Perhaps you can help us. Could you tell us what the time was when Mr Adeane returned here on Monday night?'

She spoke resentfully. 'He woke me up in the middle of the night and scared me silly.'

'Could you be more precise?'

'It was nearly three.'

'Was he sober?'

'He was anything but. Quite disgusting.'

'Now do you believe me?' Adeane demanded.

Barnard thought for a while, then said: 'Would you have any objection to providing us with one or two of your pubic hairs?'

'Would I object to *what*?'

He repeated the question.

'What d'you want them for?'

'To make comparison tests.'

Adeane's immediate reaction was to refuse. The request had to mean that foreign hairs had been found on the body or the clothes of the dead woman and therefore this was close to an accusation of guilt. Then he realized the stupidity of such reasoning. Since his hairs could not match those found, they must prove his innocence. 'All right.'

'If you would like to take Sergeant Eason . . .'

'Miss Prestley will not be embarrassed.' He unzipped his flies, took hold of several hairs and pulled.

Eason held open a small plastic bag. 'If you'd drop 'em in.' When Adeane had done that, he pressed the two rims together to seal the bag. He brought out a pen from his breast pocket, rested the bag down on the table by the side of the telephone and noted on the label contents, time, place, and his name.

'There's one last thing,' Barnard said. 'Do you know what blood group you are?'

'I think it's AB.'

'You're not certain?'

'No.'

'Thank you. We'll leave you in peace.'

As soon as Adeane had shut the front door behind them, Patricia, her voice shrill, said: 'Why did they want your JT hairs? What are they going to compare them to?'

'They're investigating the rape and murder in Colling Wood and presumably they've found some hairs on the dead woman that weren't hers and they're going to see if they're mine.'

'God Almighty, they think they could be? Why pick on you?'

'Bits of a broken rear car light were found near the body and they asked all the local garages to tell them if anyone turned up in a car with a bust pod. Someone in Lexington Garage told them about me. But when they discover my hairs don't match the ones they've found, they'll cross me off the list of suspicious characters, so there's no call for panic.'

As they returned into the sitting-room, he wondered if her expression had not been one more of calculation than concern?

The phone range at a quarter to twelve on Thursday morning. 'Mr Adeane?'

'Speaking.'

'This is Fastrack Manufacturing. Mr Fifield would like to speak to you; would you hang on one moment, please?'

This had to be one of the firms to whom he had applied for a job – but which one? To sound intelligent, he must identify it but as could happen when suddenly stressed mentally, when he needed his mind to be razor sharp, it became blunted . . . Then he had it. A medium-sized company, based just outside London, which manufactured spare parts for cars and was gaining an increasing proportion of the market.

Fifield came on the line and conducted a telephone interview. At the conclusion, he suggested a date for a face-to-face with the managing director and asked if this would be convenient? Had he named Christmas Day, it would have been convenient.

Adeane replaced the phone. He'd passed the telephone interview. This called for a celebration.

Having poured himself a drink and finished half of it, his optimism began to wane. Others would have been called, only one could be chosen. If forty really were the cut-off point that commentators (presumably younger) claimed it to be and one of the other applicants was thirty-nine . . . He drained the glass, refilled it. If a man couldn't lose a couple of years when that was necessary, he wasn't much of a PRO.

The forensic laboratory rang on Friday morning. The speaker was pedagogic in manner. As the detective inspector would no doubt understand – his speech was slow, careful, and larded with underlinings – whilst visual and mensural examination could not determine that a hair came from a certain individual – even when average diameter of medulla, pigmentation of cortex, and cross section exactly matched – it was possible to say that exhibit and comparison hairs agreed in every respect. In the Wendy Marshall case, they did so.

Further tests were to be carried out when it was hoped to make a DNA profile that would provide a degree of identification of a very high order indeed, but since these would take a considerable time, the speaker had thought the detective inspector would welcome an intermediate report.

Barnard replaced the phone on its cradle. The evidence was pointing inexorably in one direction and the more it did so, the more certain he became that it must not be accepted, yet the more pressed he became to treat it as valid.

He rang the police surgeon and asked if the other would be able to find time as soon as possible to examine Adeane's hand and take a sample of his blood? To his surprise – the doctor was known as an awkward bastard – he agreed to do so that afternoon.

Barnard rang Adeane. 'Could you drop in here – that's to say, the divisional police station – this afternoon at three-thirty?'

'Why?'

'I would like the police surgeon to examine your hand and take a blood sample.'

'And if I say to hell with the idea?'

'Then I'd wonder why you would wish to hinder our attempts to identify the murderer.'

'You make certain you have it both ways, don't you?'

'As a superintendent once said to me, that ability is the only one we share with politicians.'

The examination, held in one of the interview rooms, was brief. The doctor was a morose Scotsman. He said nothing as he examined the twin scratches on Adeane's right hand, restricted himself to a minimum of words when he asked if Adeane minded providing a sample of blood.

'Would I be here if I did?' Adeane asked, annoyed by this regard for his rights as an innocent man when the whole object of the exercise was presumably to prove him guilty.

'The taking of your blood would be a technical assault if you object,' Barnard said equably.

'As well as making you wonder why I should object.'

'You've taken the words right out of my mouth.'

Over the years, the Teerson Laboratory in east London had specialized in car traces, with the result that their expertise on identifying and matching them was sought by police forces all over the country. An assistant rang divisional HQ on Thursday to report that the exhibit slivers from a rear-light pod matched the comparison ones and due to the presence of an unusual contaminant in both, it could be stated without fear of contradiction that they came from the same batch of rear-light pods.

The manufacturers of the pods would have to be asked how many in one batch were produced and Peugeot would have to be contacted to see if they could follow these through but, Barnard decided, in the meantime the evidence from the laboratory was sufficiently strong to ask for Adeane's car to be examined for compromising traces. He thought it very likely, indeed virtually certain, that one or more would be found.

Adeane watched his car driven away on a low loader, returned into the house. Patricia met him in the hall. 'You know what it means, don't you? Your JT hairs are the same as the ones they found on her.'

'You don't think they might want my car just to check it out along with quite a few others to make certain it's clean?'

'How d'you know other cars have had broken light pods?'

'Since I was nowhere near Colling Wood that Monday night, at least one other car must have had.'

'How can you say you weren't there when you keep claiming you were too drunk to remember anything? Why did you lie to the police about being drunk at your brother-in-law's place?'

'I didn't. You confirmed that.'

'All I said was, you were digustingly drunk when you got back here. He's told them you were sober when you left his place. What did you do – get blind drunk to try to forget?'

'Your faith in me is touching. He's lying.'

'Why should he?'

'Because he's the murderer and serial rapist and he's desperately trying to divert suspicion from himself.'

'Now I've heard everything! You think a man as rich as him is going to go around raping and murdering?'

'History shows that for the rich that used to be one of the favourite pastimes on days when they couldn't hunt animals. Look, we're letting worry make us talk stupidly. You must know that sober or drunk I could never willingly hurt anyone.'

'Must I?'

'I had hoped so.'

'How were your hairs found on the dead woman if it wasn't you who raped her?'

'Could you stop jumping to conclusions?'

She turned, went into the sitting-room, slamming the door after herself.

He wondered what damned him more in her eyes – the possibility he was a rapist and murderer or his failure to be a rich man?

CHAPTER 28

'We now know that the fibre which was found in Adeane's car came from the dead woman's jersey.' Dawes stood in front of Barnard's desk. 'The pubic hairs are similar and further tests are likely to prove the overwhelming odds that those on her body came from him; the slivers of the light pod match those recovered from his car; the police doctor says the scratches on his hand are fully consistent with having been caused by someone's nails; the laboratory confirms the bloodied flesh found under the nail shows the same blood group as his and we can accept that the DNA profiling will show both flesh and blood to be virtually certain to be his; he hasn't an alibi and a witness is ready to testify that when he claims to have been blacked-out from drunkenness, he's lying –'

'A witness who has the greatest possible interest in having him arrested,' interrupted Barnard.

'You know that, I know that, but how do we prove it? We've bust our respective guts trying to prove Walker-Jones is framing Adeane and how far have we got?' He slammed his fist down on the desk. 'Bloody nowhere.'

'The proof has to be somewhere.'

'Then just tell me where in the hell it is?'

'I wish to God I could.'

Dawes jammed his hands in the pockets of his trousers and began to jingle coins. 'If the media discovers the weight of evidence we now have against Adeane, they'll crucify us for not arresting him.'

'How can we, believing him to be innocent?'

'For God's sake, stop talking naive. What we believe is of no account. It's up to us to investigate, to gather the evidence and present it to the prosecution service. It's their, and then the court's, duty to judge the value of the evidence; not ours.'

'That argument is a great way of anaesthetizing one's conscience.'

'If the investigation has been thorough and honestly conducted, there can be no call for consciences to need anaesthetizing.'

'And when Adeane is put on trial?'

'Then it's the jury who need to consider consciences.'

'But I'll be considering mine and not liking what I see and I'll lay very long odds that you'll be doing the same. Sir . . . If Adeane murdered Wendy Marshall, how come similar masking tape was used in the other cases? Especially when we can prove he can have had nothing to do with them?'

'A question the defence will put to the jury.'

'And against all the other evidence, it won't be worth a can of beans. Yet we know that that's the final proof that Adeane is innocent and has been set up.'

'If justice were administered by God, the innocent would never be found guilty, or the guilty, innocent. But it's administered by humans.' Dawes brought his hand out of his pockets, rested them on the desk and leaned forward so that his arms took his weight. 'Look, John, ignore what I've been saying and I'm a hundred and one per cent with you. But in my position I cannot ignore it and in your position, you shouldn't.'

Barnard said: 'Has the media any notion of the strength of the evidence against Adeane?'

'Judging by the number of times they call us incompetent bunglers, I doubt it.'

'Then don't arrest Adeane yet. Something may turn up.'

'Seems like I've a Micawber as a DI!'

Adeane was staring into space, his mind a cauldron of fear and self-condemnation that was exacerbated by isolation, when the front door bell rang. He went through to the hall and opened the front door to face Diana.

She spoke hurriedly. 'I know this is embarrassing for you, but I must have a word.'

'About Melly?'

She shook her head. 'About you.'

'Come on in.'

'We can talk in my car if that'll be easier?'

'Patricia's not around, so if you've no objection to coming in, enter.'

She stepped into the hall. He led the way into the sitting-room. She began to speak as she sat. 'Melly and I have been staying with Mother and only returned home last night. Serena rang me an hour ago and said . . .' She stopped.

'Probably that I am the rapist and murderer?'

'How can even she be that absurd? How can she repeat such wicked nonsense?'

'She doesn't believe it to be nonsense.'

'For God's sake, Dick, I'm too upset to enjoy your twisted sense of humour.'

'I'm not trying to be funny.'

'You . . . you're saying that the police really think you could have something to do with that ghastly murder?'

'Not just something. Everything.'

'Then they're a pack of bloody fools.' She spoke vehemently.

'I wonder if you can have any idea what it means at last to find someone who believes in me.'

'Anyone who knows you, must. Surely . . . She must believe you?'

He shook his head. 'Patricia is very much a fair-weather sailor. She headed back to port the moment the storm appeared over the horizon.'

'You mean . . .'

'She has a strongly developed sense of self-preservation, so she's cleared out in good time.'

'I'm sorry.'

'I'm not.'

They were silent for a while, then she said: 'Will you tell me all that's happened?'

He did so.

She fiddled with the belt on her dress. 'So when you named Tom as the rapist, you were right?'

'As he's done his damnedest to incriminate me, I have to be . . . I know you regard loyalty to one's family as all important and that to betray such loyalty is one of the worst things one can do, but I really did believe I was faced by conflicting duties. I didn't name Tom to the police because I was jealous and trying to get my own back on him, I did it because I genuinely believed he might be the rapist and murderer and by naming him I might be saving other women from becoming victims.'

'I can see that now.'

'Then . . .' He hesitated, spoke in a rush, his voice harsh: 'Then you can also see how I condemned Wendy Marshall to death.'

'That's absurd!'

'If I hadn't named him, he'd not have raped and murdered her in order to try to incriminate me.'

'You did what you believed you had to do and couldn't possibly foresee what the consequences would be. So stop blaming yourself for something totally outside your control . . . How are you going to make the police understand you had nothing to do with her death?'

'A good question.'

'Answer it.'

'I can't.'

'You've got to.'

'There's so much evidence against me, it's incredible I wasn't arrested some time ago.'

'Obviously they know you're not guilty.'

'The pubic hairs were mine, the skin under the dead woman's nail was mine, the broken bits of light pod were from my car, there's an incriminating trace in the car, I've no alibi, Tom's named me a liar . . . The Recording Angel would be hard pushed to believe me innocent.'

'The proof of your innocence has to be somewhere,' she said, almost angrily, unknowingly echoing what Barnard had said.

*   *   *

179

Just as she had a far stronger sense of loyalty than most, Diana had a stronger belief in a rigid honesty; she abhorred the modern, pragmatic view of what was right and wrong. But because she was no fanatic, even when supporting what she so firmly believed, she accepted that exceptionally there could be a case when the ends justified the means; the use of violence, whether physical or mental, was normally barbaric, but there were wrongs which could only be righted by barbaric means, a fact that was proven by a defensive war.

On Monday morning she went up to London by train and in turn visited five shops, none of which was able to supply her with what she sought. But her growing pessimism was dismissed when the sixth shop, noted for the unusual animals it stocked and sold, said they did have a tarantula – at double the maximum price she had expected.

Back home by 1.30, she put the boxed spider on the table by the telephone and went to lift the receiver, then withdrew her hand. Even though she had already asked herself the same question over and over again, she now asked it once more. Could anything justify her proposed action, since it was designed to bring terror to someone to whom she owed the duty of family love? The answer hadn't altered. Yes, if to do so saved possible future victims, even if she owed them no direct duty, and if she could restore innocence to someone in grave danger of being falsely declared guilty. She tapped the cardboard box four times, her magic number, lifted the receiver, dialled.

Pablo, whose pronunciation seemed to have taken a sharp turn for the worse, said Señora Walky-Hones was eating . . .

Serena, using a cordless phone, cut in. 'Who is it?'

'Di. Sorry to interrupt lunch.'

'It's not a proper meal. I'm starving myself on salad and a fat-reduced cheese which tastes filthy. Thomas has been moaning that I've been putting on weight.'

'Tell him that the thin die young and unsatisfied. In any case, surely he knows you could eat the Ritz empty and not ring up another ounce . . . Are you doing anything this afternoon?'

'Nothing special.'

'I thought you'd like to hear how Mother is in greater detail than I told you over the phone.'

'Yes, I would,' Serena answered, not very convincingly.

'Will Tom be in – wouldn't want to bore him with unalloyed domesticity.'

'He's phoned to say he can't be back before eight at the earliest because of work. I've had to tell Juanita we won't be eating until nine.'

'Won't such a break with tradition cause mental disorientation?'

'I don't know why you think it's so odd we should keep to a routine.'

'Because I enjoy the unexpected . . . I'll be along at three, then.' Diana rang off. She patted the box four times.

CHAPTER 29

Serena opened the front door. 'It's their afternoon off,' she said, to explain why she was acting as doorman.

'Is it?' replied Diana vaguely, as if she had not known that.

'That's the trouble with staff these days; they demand so much free time they're hardly ever here.' As Diana stepped into the hall, Serena's acquisitive gaze centred on the wrapped parcel her sister was carrying.

'A little surprise for you.' Then, as Serena held out her hand, Diana added: 'You'll have to wait a little.'

'I hate waiting.'

'Sometimes it turns out to be an advantage.'

'You're being very mysterious.'

'I saw a third grey hair in the mirror this morning and decided that now the only possible weapon left in my armoury is to be mysterious.'

'You're talking nonsense.'

'Mimsy borogroves?'

'For heaven's sake, are you tight, or something?'

'Something.'

'Come on,' Serena said, annoyed because she thought her sister was making fun of her.

They crossed the hall and made their way through to the Regent's Room. As soon as she was settled, Serena said: 'Isn't it horrible about Richard? It's going to be so shame-making for us. I mean, people will say we're related, even if he's only your ex, or nearly ex. You'll divorce him as soon as you can, won't you?'

'I hadn't thought about it.'

'But you must. As Thomas said, it's the only way we can all distance ourselves from him.'

'Then Tom's no doubts about Dick's guilt?'

'How can he after the way he made those terrible accusations and with all the inquiries the police have been making?'

'Yet he's not been arrested.'

'Thomas says that's only because the police are so completely incompetent they haven't yet collated all the evidence. He reckons that if they were a commercial firm, they'd have gone bankrupt years ago.'

'He sounds as if he's worried that the police aren't satisfied Dick really is guilty and are trying to prove his innocence. I mean, Tom's not in the clear unless and until Dick is arrested, is he?'

Serena stared at her sister, her expression changing from surprise to anger. 'My God, you're trying to . . . You're like Dick. You're so jealous of us you'll say anything beastly if you think it'll hurt.'

'How much of the truth do you know?'

'You're not going to sit there and make filthy accusations. Clear out and don't bother ever to come back.'

'I'll go when I have the answers.'

'I'll have you thrown out.'

'You seem to forget Pablo's away.' She stood, the parcel in her right hand. 'You do realize, do you, that if you don't tell the police all you know or suspect, they may never be able to show that Dick's innocent and so he'll be tried, found guilty, and imprisoned?'

'It's nothing to do with me.'

'It's everything to do with you. For once, you've got to look at what you're seeing. You provided Tom with a false alibi, didn't you?'

'I got back here just before ten.'

'From where?'

'London.'

'What did you do there?'

'I did some shopping and went to the cinema. But what's it . . . ?'

'You haven't been to the cinema in years because you

183

think it's common; you only go to the theatre. Where were you? With friends?'

'I was in London!' Serena shouted.

'All those years ago, Mother said to me that she always knew when you were lying because you looked away when you promised you were telling the truth. You looked away just now. You're going to give me their names so that the police can find out exactly when you left their place.'

'Clear out of here.'

'There's something even more important than Dick's innocence at stake. The women who'll be raped and murdered if Tom's not locked away.'

'You've gone mad.'

'You won't tell me who the friends were and anything else you know?'

'I won't tell you a bloody thing. But Thomas will, when he gets back. He'll sue you for libel.'

'Slander, as Dick would pedantically correct you.' Diana unwrapped the parcel. 'I was hoping to God I wouldn't have to do this.' She lifted the lid and stared down at the massive, hairy spider. Prompted by the light, it tentatively moved a couple of legs, and although she had no fear of spiders and knew this one to be harmless, when it appeared to fix its gaze on her, she knew brief, primitive fear. She remembered Serena at the age of four, screaming because she'd brushed into a web and the spider had landed on her arm; when eight, being driven home in hysterics because one of the boys at the party had tried to drop a spider down her neck; when sixteen, attending several aversion-therapy sessions and ironically suffering an increased phobia.

Diana accepted that she might well be about to cause her sister damaging mental distress that could be permanent, yet she moved forward and held the box so that Serena could see what was in it. 'Tell me everything or I'll put this on your head.'

After a few seconds, Serena began to scream; her terror was so great that she involuntarily urinated.

*　　　*　　　*

Had Serena, terrified beyond reason, not told Diana what she had seen, no one would ever have suspected that the small collections of stones marked graves; they were not in any geometric order and were therefore apparently of no significance, even though the ground was not very stony.

There were five such scatterings. Since Wendy Marshall had been forced off her Vespa and physically overcome, and had not been lured into a car by the impression of trust-worthiness that a friendly dog provided, it seemed obvious that the fifth grave must contain the body of a dog used in a rape, or a rape and murder, hitherto unconnected – for what reason not yet known – with the others.

Two PCs, in shirt-sleeves because, although it was well into the evening, it was still warm, were excavating the pen-ultimate grave. The photographer and SOCO waited nearby, Dawes and Barnard a little further back.

Dawes said: 'You think the wife really didn't put two and two together?'

'I reckon she's the kind of person who only sees what she wants to see and understands only what she wants to understand,' Barnard replied. 'When she came back that day from the holiday on her own and saw his car was in the garage but he wasn't around, went to look for him and found him burying a dog, she should have begun to suspect. But his explanation that he'd unfortunately run it over and hadn't wanted to leave it in the road like a piece of rubbish, allowed her to believe the matter to be without any significance.'

'And later, when she saw another collection of stones?'

'She'll have taken great care not to return to this part of the park for fear that if she did, she'd no longer be able to hide the truth from herself.'

'You're making her mind to be as twisted as his.'

'At least hers hasn't driven her to murder.'

'There's something about the dogs being buried here I don't understand. Why didn't he just let 'em go; or kill them and dump 'em somewhere where they wouldn't mean any-thing? And why have the graves close together when he'd the whole park to choose from; and why mark them with stones?'

'I'd say he wanted them together and marked so he could come and look at them, know the dogs were buried there and so heighten the pleasure of recall. It's a fairly common habit of sexual criminals to keep mementoes to fuel their memories. And he must have judged it virtually impossible for anyone else to understand the true significance of the stones.'

Dawes watched a butterfly zigzag past him. 'Thank God I don't know if you're right or wrong ... We can prove he lied about his wife's returning at ten and that strips him of any alibi. We can prove dogs have been buried here and although so far there's nothing to identify any of 'em, we're hoping one of the two remaining graves contains the dog stolen from Mrs Harvey in Kington because that had an electronic-tag implant which will give a positive identification. That'll link him to the rape of Eve Ritchie. Yet since the last grave can't contain the body of a dog to tie him in with Wendy Marshall's murder, where's the proof that he murdered her and planted the evidence on Adeane?'

'Unless he confesses – and with his character, is he likely to do that? – it looks like it'll be a question of asking the jury to draw the correct assumption.'

'I pray my innocence never rests on a jury having sufficient intelligence to be able to do that.'

'We can show he'd every reason to try to incriminate Adeane; we can show Adeane can't have had any connection with the other rapes or murder . . .'

'Here we are!' one of the PCs called out.

They went forward and stared down at the white, wiry hairs which had been revealed. Dawes gestured to the SOCO.

His hands in surgical gloves, the SOCO used a scalpel and brush with all the slow, methodical care of an archaeologist excavating some ancient artefact to remove the earth from around the body, putting this earth into a plastic bag. When the body was free, he lifted it up and on to an opened animal body-bag. 'West Highland White,' he said. 'I've a cousin who breeds 'em.' He showed them the end of a length of string which wound around the neck. 'Strangled, like the rest of the poor little sods.'

'Can you feel an implant in the neck?' Dawes asked.

The SOCO prodded the neck, his expression making it clear how unwelcome a task this was in view of the state of decomposition. 'There's something under the skin here which feels the size of a pea.'

'That'll be it. OK. Seal up.'

'We've got him by the short and curlies,' Barnard said.

'Sure, but that's only half the problem solved. I'm a bloody sight less optimistic than you are that we'll be able to sort out the other half.' He spoke to the PCs. 'Dig up the last grave.'

Because the ground had recently been disturbed, the task was relatively easy and before long the hole was a foot deep, yet none of the other dogs had been buried under a greater depth of soil than six inches.

'Looks like it's empty,' said the elder PC. 'All ready for the next one, maybe.'

Barnard stepped forward and looked down into the hole. 'How's the soil at the bottom – packed solid or still loose?'

'Still a bit loose.'

'Keep digging.'

The order was not, as the PCs made obvious without ever descending into dumb insolence, a welcome one. They continued digging, alternately as there was not room for them both to do so at the same time, until the younger man stopped and said, as he felt the earth: 'There's something here.'

'Leave it.' Barnard waited until they'd moved back, then called the SOCO over.

The SOCO knelt, began to scoop out the soil with his hand, placing that in another plastic bag. After a moment, he brought up an object, some ten inches long, thin, and judging from the patches that were free of earth, made of metal.

'What is it?' Dawes asked.

'Can't rightly say, sir, but it seems like it's nothing more than a comb.' His tone was angry from disappointment; as had all present, he'd been hoping against hope that there would be the proof that was needed.

It was Barnard who first realized what they might be looking at. 'It's a curry-comb.'

'What's that?'

'Used for grooming horses. Wendy Marshall was on her way back from the stables, so she'll likely have been carrying gear with her, not wanting it to be nicked. There wasn't any dog for that bastard to bury to feed his sick memories, so maybe he took the curry-comb.'

Dawes said: 'Clear off the earth and see if there are any distinguishing marks on it.'

The SOCO arranged a sheet of plastic on the ground, tapped the stainless-steel comb until it was almost clean, then used a small brush to ease off what earth remained.

'Are there any marks?' Dawes demanded, revealing the tension within him by asking the unnecessary question, since the other was already visually examining the curry-comb, holding it by the edge.

'Can't see any maker's mark, number, or anything,' said the SOCO.

'Shit!'

'But hang on.' He held the comb a little closer. 'Looks like there are several coarse hairs caught up in the teeth.'

'And DNA profiling should be able to match them to her horse. Just not quite clever enough to think of everything,' Barnard said, with deep satisfaction.

August weather was typically unstable, but the last day of the month was bright. Adeane stepped out of his car into the hot sunshine, walked through the garden and round to the front door. Diana opened this as he approached and Amelia rushed past her to hug him. He said to Diana, speaking over Amelia's head: 'I was wondering if you'd anything fixed up for the day?'

'Nothing that can't be altered.'

'Then what do you say to lunch somewhere?'

'Yes,' said Amelia.

'Yes, please,' corrected Diana automatically. 'Is there a

special reason or just the joys of autumn?' she asked him.

'I had an interview yesterday afternoon.'

'And?'

'They offered me the job.'

'Oh, Dick! I've been so hoping and hoping for you.'

When he saw how genuine was her pleasure, felt the increased hug of Amelia, his hopes grew stronger that because Diana had been forced to learn the bitter truth that loyalties, however exemplary, must sometimes be betrayed, she would be able to find sufficient sympathy for his betrayal of their marriage to welcome him back.